Hel

All roads lead

With very best wishes

Richard

THE ROLLING STONES IN SHEFFIELD

Richard Crooks

First published by Arc Publishing 2023

Arc Publishing
56 Heather Lea Avenue
Dore
Sheffield S17 3DL

Printed by Bayliss Print

Text copyright Richard Crooks 2023

Every effort has been made to trace copyright holders and obtain their permission for the use of copyright material. The author apologises for any oversights and would be grateful for notification of any corrections that should be incorporated in future reprints or editions of this book.

All rights reserved. No part of this book may be reproduced, sold or utilised in any form or by any means, electronic or mechanical, including photocopying, recording or by any information storage and retrieval system, without prior permission in writing from the Author.

All views and comments in this book are those of the author and should not be attributed to the publisher.

A CIP catalogue record is available for this book from the British Library.

ISBN: 9781906722968

For my granddaughter Dorothy Pauline – the greatest band you could ever wish to see

Contents

Acknowledgements

Preface

Foreword

1.	The 1960s…..The Beatles….and The Rolling Stones	8
2.	Monday 22nd October 1963 – Gaumont (two shows)	15
3.	Wednesday 13th November 1963 – City Hall	20
4.	Thursday 27th February 1964 – City Hall (two shows)	25
5.	Friday 29th May 1964 – City Hall (two shows)	30
6.	Thursday 11th March 1965 – City Hall (two shows)	34
7.	Chat With Dave Berry	44
8.	Monday 11th October 1965 – Gaumont (two shows)	47
9.	Between Times – 1965 – 1995	59
10.	Sunday 9th July 1995 – Don Valley Stadium	62
11.	Sunday 6th June 1999 – Don Valley Stadium	80
12.	Sunday 27th August 2006 – Don Valley Stadium	92
13.	Since 2006	105
14.	The Venues	107

Bibliography

Acknowledgements

I'd like to thank Editor Claire Lewis at the *Sheffield Star* for giving me permission to quote from the newspaper – the newspaper provides the main contemporary reports in the book – and for the use of their images in this book.

Thank you to Jane Salt, Librarian at the *Sheffield Star* for her assistance and patience in tracking down the images from that newspaper used in the book.

And to Jennifer Mannion of the *Sheffield Star* for producing a first-rate article about the book, resulting in contact being made with people about their recollections of seeing The Rolling Stones in Sheffield.

In particular I'd like to thank Dave Berry for giving me his time and his recollections of touring in the 1960s with The Rolling Stones.

To Matt Lee my gratitude for his assistance and images from his unparalleled collection of Rolling Stones memorabilia – reflected in his definitive book, *Hot Stuff The Story Of The Rolling Stones Through The Ultimate Memorabilia Collection* (Welbeck, 2021).

To Kim Ward for her recollections of meeting Mick Jagger off stage before the show at the Don Valley Stadium in 1999.

To the staff at the British Library – and particularly those in the Newsroom – whose continued patience with a technically challenged author, were of the greatest assistance in helping me work through all the microfiche research.

Arc Publishing, thank you to Chris Keeling for his expertise in designing the cover and producing the book.

And to Jennifer Ann Wiles and Julian Crooks for their thoughts and suggestions - all the remaining imperfections are my responsibility.

Preface

There are hundreds of books about The Rolling Stones. Books covering a myriad of topics - tours, the early days, band members and so much more. They include books about The Rolling Stones in America, New York, Germany and Scandinavia. But there are none about The Rolling Stones in Sheffield. And that's a gap in the literature this book is intended to fill.

Why write about The Rolling Stones?

And why Sheffield?

For me the answers are simple and straight-forward.

I have a real passion for The Rolling Stones, their music, their stage performances and all they stand for. I've had that passion since I was a young lad in the 1960s growing up in Sheffield, my home city.

Foreword

The Rolling Stones have played an estimated 2250 shows in their career to date. 14 of those shows in Sheffield – the first in 1963, the most recent in 2006.

This book has those shows at its core – the venues, the build-up, the support artists, the performances – contemporary reports and memories of people who were there, and any particular events associated with the shows.

The most recent record releases by the band at the date of each show are identified.

Added to that the social and historical context of the time is brought out – including the headline of the local evening newspaper, *The Star*, on the day of the show.

The book fills in the details of The Rolling Stones tours, performances and major events, between their visits to the steel city and thereafter.

Chapter 1

The 1960s….The Beatles…and The Rolling Stones

A different time, a different era. In cultural terms the 1960s are the proverbial light years away from the present day.

The Second World War had ended less than a decade and a half before the start of the 1960s. Britain was recovering from the privations and losses of that conflict. A society that was essentially deferential. A society where teenagers had only just begun to make their presence felt.

The music scene had developed slowly at first until the arrival in the 1950s in the USA of Elvis Presley, Little Richard, Jerry Lee Lewis and Bill Haley and the Comets amongst others. In this country the trad jazz scene was supplanted with the arrival of skiffle – Lonnie Donegan a pre-eminent exponent, and the music that followed - Marty Wilde, Cliff Richard and the Shadows, Joe Brown and the Bruvvers - all part of the evolving music scene in the late 1950s moving into the following decade.

But it was the arrival of The Beatles onto the music scene and into the charts in 1962 that changed everything. They stormed to the top of those charts worldwide, their pop music the fresh sound of a new generation. Teenagers loved them, Mums and Dads embraced them. They looked good in their neatly cut suits and well-trimmed hair. The so-called "Fab Four". They appeared on light entertainment programmes and quickly became part of an established order, albeit an order that was changing as the decade progressed.

And then came The Rolling Stones. They were different. Very different. Their music rhythm and blues at its core. They had no time for established norms. Their attitude and approach? Rebels. They didn't give a f**k. They dressed how they wanted to. Their hair as long and as unkempt as they wanted it. The very antithesis of The Beatles. They were the "bad boys" and played up to that role.

Hair was a big thing in the 1960s – short back and sides or the neatly trimmed mop-tops that The Beatles sported were fine. Long hair, unkempt hair…absolutely not the done thing.

And that resonated with me at the local barber on Artisan View in Heeley, Sheffield, Fred Wood's establishment – his offering and price list included "Long Hair Renovating" – an emphasis on the word "renovating", and as the dictionary describes it, "repairing and improving."

Interesting that Mr. Wood charged more for this haircut than any other – hardly an encouragement for would-be customers.

Making national headlines in 1964 a school in Coventry suspended eleven male pupils for having hairstyles similar to those of the Rolling Stones. The school's Headmaster confirmed they would not be welcomed back until their hair was "cut neatly, like the Beatles."

More negative comments in the country's best-selling Sunday newspaper at the time, the *News of the World*, Alan Whittaker commented, "The Stones leer rather than smile. They don't wear natty clothes. They glower. Nobody would accuse them of radiating charm. The extraordinary thing is that more and more youngsters are turning towards them. How true is this carefully nourished picture of 5 indolent morons? They give the feeling that they really enjoy wallowing in a swill-tub of their own repulsiveness." (November 1964).

The author and jazz singer George Melly had these observations about the Stones, "..they could grow their hair, cultivate a funky grubbiness, swear, behave with a consistent lack of couth, and Jagger had his big red lips going for him too. He could get by as a bogyman for the nine-till-five dads with teenage daughters." (*Revolt Into Style,* George Melly, Penguin, 1970).

Ronnie Bennett, a singer with the group the Ronettes, saw it like this, "The Beatles were just four guys who stood there with their guitars. The Stones were always different: more of a threat. They did gutsy things on stage."

The Beatles – they were safe, a little cheeky at times, but fundamentally safe. The Rolling Stones anything but safe – they were a real threat, a threat to morality. And that threat seemed to grow and grow as the decade wore on.

Andrew Oldham, the Stones manager through to the mid-1960s, observed, "The Beatles were divined and the Stones became your best hope from hell, your parent's nightmare..." (*The Stones A History In Cartoons*, Bill Wyman, Sutton Publishing, 2006).

In Sheffield our knowledge of The Beatles, The Rolling Stones and their music was based mainly on the recently created television programmes of the day – BBC's *Top of the Pops* and ITV's *Ready Steady Go,* and on radio, the BBC's Light Programme. Newspapers and magazines underscored that knowledge with the groups' off-stage activities as well as producing posters that many a youngster had on their bedroom walls.

Packs of collectable "Pop Stars" cards – with chewing gum – were in vogue at school for a while in the mid-1960s, The Rolling Stones featuring prominently. They made a change from the ever-popular collectable football cards that boys traded enthusiastically in the schoolyard.

And at Anns Road Primary School in Sheffield any straw poll taken over the period 1963-1967 would have the girls predominantly aligning their affection and appreciation with The Beatles, and the boys with The Rolling Stones.

In those days you were always asked – Beatles or Rolling Stones? One or the other – not both. A clear polarisation. The media – the newspapers in particular – had an insatiable appetite for the comparison. In October 1964, *The Star,* had the front-page headline, "It's The Beatles versus The Rolling Stones".

The headline promoted the monthly *Pop Stars Special* paper to be published for the coming weekend, commenting that the new edition "gives the views of many teenagers on which they consider the best – The Beatles or The Stones? See if you agree."

Nearly forty years later in a special edition of the *Radio Times* Danny Kelly wrote, "The groups provided two possible paths through life. The Beatles were seen as sunny and loveable, their arms and hearts wide open to all the new influences that the brave new world was offering. The Stones, in contrast, were aloof and brooding, cocking a snook to square society and celebrating nothing unless it conformed to their dark, sexually driven vision…The Stones attitude? They were curled-lip misanthropes, haughty and rude." (*Radio Times,* 23-29 August 2003).

In the same issue the *Radio Times* asked celebrities of the day their preference – Beatles or Stones? Lining up for The Beatles - Fiona Bruce, Craig David, John Humphrys, Sandi Toksvig, Monty Don and Julie Walters, and for The Stones – Ricky Gervais, Boy George, Rod Liddle, Phil Jupitus, Chris Tarrant and Mark Radcliffe.

Each had a short paragraph explaining the reasons for their choice. Chris Tarrant observed, "I was a huge Beatles fan until my parents suddenly decided to like them. And then I immediately switched my allegiance because the whole point of being a pop fan was not to like the music that your mum and dad liked. Mum's going "Well, actually they're quite nice boys, Paul speaks well." And the Stones arrived and we all became Stones fans."

And Rod Liddle, "The Stones were always magnificently debauched and, with *Let It Bleed* and *Sticky Fingers*, unsurpassable.

Chris Tarrant's observation struck a chord with me and many others - The Rolling Stones achieved greater prominence and appreciation because parents very definitely preferred The Beatles to The Rolling Stones. Certainly, the case with my Dad who had little if any time for The Rolling Stones; he considered The Beatles music would be played in fifty years' time, by which time the Stones would be long forgotten.

Underlining that fixation of The Beatles or The Rolling Stones, this extract from a 1965 Irish television interview with Mick Jagger is illuminating:

Interviewer: "How do you compare your group with the Beatles?"

Mick Jagger: "I don't know. How do you compare it with the Beatles? I don't compare it at all – there's no point."

Interviewer: "Well let's get right down to brass tacks. Do you think you're better than they are?"

Mick Jagger: "At what? You know it's not the same group. So, we just do what we want and they do what they want. You can prefer us to them or them to us."

The interviewer continues to flounder...asking if The Rolling Stones are better at what they prefer to do than the Beatles are at what they prefer to do.... the emphasis focussed on a clear distinction between the two, with the interviewer trying – and failing – to get an answer to which is the better group.

As the 1960s progressed – the Beatles last tour was in 1965 – my family moved to Gleadless, a suburb of Sheffield in 1967. And we heard rumours that Mick Jagger had been seen in the village of Eckington visiting his grandmother – just over the border in Derbyshire, Eckington was less than three miles from where we lived. But hardly worth a visit on the very off chance we might see the Rolling Stones' frontman.

Years later it became clear Mick Jagger had visited Eckington – his paternal grandmother had lived at an address on the High Street in the village, passing away in 1976.

Fourteen years earlier in 1962 The Rolling Stones – Mick Jagger, Keith Richards, Brian Jones, Charlie Watts and Bill Wyman - first saw the light of day.

I could not say with any precision when I first heard their name or their music. But it would not be long before the world had heard their name, their music, and tried to come to terms with their appearance and all they seemed to represent.

The image of the rebel, non-conformist Stones was encouraged by their young manager Andrew Loog Oldham. No issues from his perspective that they were seen as the polar opposites of the perceived nice boy Beatles, the scrapes with authority, the negative headlines – including, "Would You Let Your Daughter Marry A Rolling Stone?" (For most parents the answer would be a resounding "no" - albeit the question never asked was "Would a Rolling Stone want to marry your daughter?").

And all of this before a consideration of the music. Both groups were very successful. Again, to underline the contrast between the two groups - The Beatles' amorous intentions with the opposite sex encapsulated in their song "I Wanna Hold Your Hand"….whilst The Rolling Stones complained they "Can't Get No Satisfaction."

The author Nik Cohn has this assessment of The Rolling Stones, "The best thing about the Stones, the most important, was their huge sense of independence, uncompromised.

...The Stones were a teenage industry all by themselves, self-contained, and the adult world simply wasn't relevant. That's why they were so loathed inside the business, because they threatened the structure, because they threatened the way in which pop was controlled by old men, by men over thirty.

That's why they mattered...because they meant that you didn't need to soften up to make it any more. You didn't need to be pretty, you didn't need to simper or drool or suck up – the old men might hate you in every way possible and you could still make yourself a million dollars.

Really the Stones were major liberators: they stirred up a whole new mood of teen arrogance here...For the first time England had something like a private teen society going and, myself, I think it was the Stones rather than the Beatles who led it....the Stones were the final group of the sixties and their image was the final image, Jagger was the final face and their records were the final records." (*Awopbopaloobop Alopbamboom,* Paladin, 1970).

The Rolling Stones were edgy, and different - so, so different.

Chapter 2

Monday October 22nd 1963

Gaumont Theatre

Two Shows – 6.30pm and 8.45pm

Don Arden Enterprises Ltd Present….

The first shows The Rolling Stones ever performed in Sheffield.

They were fourth on the bill supporting The Everly Brothers, Bo Diddley and Little Richard. Add Julie Grant, Mickie Most, The Flintstones and compere Bob Bain to complete the line-up.

Part of a British tour comprising of 30 dates over 36 days, which began on 29th September at the New Victoria Theatre in London and finished at London's Hammersmith Odeon theatre on 3rd November.

The tour was advertised as the Everly Brothers – Bo Diddley Show. Disappointing box office returns at the early dates prompted the promoters to bring in a star "Special Added Attraction" – the dynamic Little Richard joined the tour after five dates. The added attraction gave the tour and ticket sales the added impetus the promoters were looking for.

At the Gaumont Theatre in the centre of Sheffield (principally used as a cinema) the price of tickets ranged from 8s. 6d (42.5p) in the Rear Circle to 15s. 0d (75p) in the Front Stalls and Front Circle. Seats were also available in the Rear Stalls for 10s. 0d (50p) and 12s. 6d (62.5p) in the Centre Stalls and Centre Circle.

The songs from which the Stones selected for their ten minutes slot in the show – *Poison Ivy, Fortune Teller, Come On, Money, Talkin' About You* later adding *I Wanna Be Your Man, Road Runner, and Memphis Tennessee.*

Referring to the appearance of the Stones, Phil Everly commented, "They were just bringing in that not-dressing-for-the-stage and they looked quite peculiar, but they did a good job. They stood out. They were an easy bunch of guys to be around but they kept to themselves as well."

In the following morning's *Sheffield Telegraph* a review of the show appeared under the headline, "Rock 'n roll spirit all over again it's fun."

The reviewer – "C.N." – titled the review, "The Everly Brothers Show":

"It could have been Gipsy Rose Lee – but it was actually Little Richard, stripping to the waist and distributing the spoils – tie, shirt and shoes – among a frenzied audience at the Gaumont, Sheffield, last night.

Bo Diddley, the nearest to real R&B we've ever seen in Sheffield, wasn't as wild as some of our own local groups, turning out a highly commercialised performance which I found rather disappointing.

He wasn't really on long enough to get warmed up.

For the wildest act of the evening, it was a toss-up between:

Little Richard, turning the clock back with oldies like *Rip It Up* and *Lucille* but proving he's just as great as ever….

…. And the Rolling Stones, a raving beat group who make The Beatles sound as select as the Palm Court Orchestra.

Stars of the show, the inimitable Everly Brothers, sounded as sweet and soulful as ever - a joy to listen to.

Singing some of their million-plus sellers – *Cathy's Clown, So Sad* – they were superb."

Interesting to note again the comparison with The Beatles, even at this early stage in their career.

The running order of the show – The Flintstones, Bob Bain (Compere), Mickie Most, The Rolling Stones, Little Richard, Interval, Julie Grant, Bo Diddley, The Everly Brothers

On the tour the Stones generally received a good response from the audience.

A fan who attended the Sheffield concert had these comments on the evening's entertainment:

"It was a great show….The Everly's were outstanding that night....They played a whole load of their hits and ended the show with *Cathy's Clown* to a standing ovation and then came back on stage and did it again for an encore

...The Rolling Stones were a little known group in 1963 with only one record just in the charts, it was a Chuck Berry song called *Come On* (It only got to Number 21) .....On the night they only performed two numbers the first was Chuck Berry's *Talking About You* followed by their first release ... I thought they were too loud…."

Other recollections of the show include:

"The thing that sticks in my memory was the fact that they were all dressed in black and white dogtooth suits. I don't think I ever recall seeing them after that time appearing in suits." - David Roe

"The Stones looked great and their performance was fantastic - what we could hear of it." - Bob Miller (both quoted in *You Had To Be There The Rolling Stones Live 1962-69,* Richard Houghton, Gottahavebooks, 2015).

It was reported the Stones were paid £1275 for the 30 nights' tour (60 shows). This worked out to £42 10s. (£42.50) for each night or £21 5s. (£21.25) for each show (as referenced in *Rolling With The Stones,* Bill Wyman, Dorling Kindersley, 2002).

In the same book, Bill Wyman commented, "After the show in Sheffield we went out on the town and found a coffee bar. We were talking to a couple of local lads when a crowd formed outside. The old guy who ran the coffee bar didn't know who we were and, not wanting trouble, threw us out. We had to make a run for it back to our hotel."

Keith Richards' observations on that first tour: "Little Richard, Bo Diddley, The Everly Brothers and a few other weirdo acts like us thrown in for good measure. What an education – like going to Rock 'n' Roll university – six weeks working with these guys every night."

And Mick Jagger, "I used to spend a lot of time with Little Richard. He used to teach me a lot…I would watch him every single night to see how he handled the audience. He was a great audience manipulator, in the best sense of the word. I probably learned more from him than anyone else."

The next date on the tour was the following night at the Odeon Theatre Nottingham.

The Rolling Stones' first single, *Come On*, had been released four months earlier on 7th June 1963 – peaked at Number 21 and stayed in the charts for 14 weeks.

And what was being reported locally on the day of the show? The front-page headline in *The Star* a broadsheet sized newspaper priced at 4d (1.5p) – "7 Killed In Jet Crash" with the strapline "Britain's One-Eleven burst into flames after plunge".

Readers learnt that all seven on-board Britain's "bus stop" airliner died when it crashed on a test flight over Wiltshire – the victims test pilots and observers in the British Aircraft Corporation's short haul jet "which is carrying much of Britain's hopes in the export markets."

In the following day's newspaper, front page headline: "City Rag team scrap plot to kidnap Beatles" the article highlighted, "Sheffield University Rag Committee have decided to abandon the "snatch" after writing to The Beatles to ask them: "Will it be all right if we kidnap you on Rag Day?"

Chapter 3

Wednesday 13 November 1963

City Hall (Oval Hall)

Presented and Compered by The Stringfellow Bros.

A tour beginning on 4 November 1963 at the Top Rank Ballroom in Preston and finishing on 5th January 1964 at the Ricky Tick, Olympic Ballroom in Reading. They played 58 shows in 62 days. And all this touring up and down the country with Ian Stewart – the 6th Stone - driving the group in his Volkswagen van!

And the touring was gruelling – Bill Wyman recollected, "If we arrived back really late, which was quite often if we were coming down from say, Sheffield or Manchester, we might get to my place (in London) at about three in the morning." (*Stu*, Will Nash, Out-Take Limited, 2003).

So little more than three weeks after their first appearance in Sheffield, the Rolling Stones were back in the city and headlining at the City Hall. One Show – "The R & B Show" - with an advertised timing of 7.30pm to 11pm.

On the same bill – The Big Three, Wayne Fontana and the Mindbenders, The Sheffields, The Vantennas, Johnny Tempest and the Cadillacs, Karen Young, Vance Arnold And The Avengers and The Four Plus One. Nine performers in one show. And Vance Arnold? – none other than the city's own Joe Cocker.

Bill Wyman's recollection of the show – "In Sheffield, we again wore casual clothes and played to 3000 fans. It was a wild crowd and we had a really great show." (*Rolling With The Stones*, Dorling Kindersley, 2002).

By the date of the show the Rolling Stones had appeared a total of three times on national television – twice on ITV's *Thank Your Lucky*

Stars (July and September 1963) and on *Ready Steady Go* (August 1963), on each occasion performing *Come On*, their first single record.

The show was promoted and compered by the local "Stringfellow Bros" – the soon to be nationally famous Peter Stringfellow and his younger brother Geoffrey. Earlier that year the Stringfellows had been the promoters for the first appearance of The Beatles in the city – at the Azena Ballroom on White Lane, Gleadless (now a Co-op store).

Tickets for the show priced at 4/-, 5/-, 6/- (20p, 25p, 30p) were available from either of the local Stringfellows clubs - Black Cat Club, Blue Moon Club or from the music store Wilson Peck on the corner of Leopold Street and Barkers Pool in the city centre. Ticket prices notably lower for this show – it lacked the big star names from the United States.

In his autobiography Stringfellow recollects his meeting with The Rolling Stones at the City Hall, "Mick Jagger may sometimes give the impression that he is "all right, mate" friendliness, but he isn't a bit like that. In fact, I'd never met anyone like him before. I paid the Stones £125 and I was the one pulling them on stage, yet he couldn't even be bothered to speak to me. I remember going up to the dressing room in Sheffield and seeing Brian Jones and Mick Jagger having an intense conversation. They didn't want to talk to me or anyone else, so I left them to it." (*Kings of Clubs*, Peter Stringfellow with Fiona Lafferty, Little, Brown and Company, 1996).

Vance Arnold and the Avengers played four numbers including the Arthur Alexander penned *You Better Move On* - the slow downbeat song was recorded by the Stones at De Lane Lea Recording Studios, London the day after the Sheffield show and released in January 1964 on *The Rolling Stones* EP. Interesting to speculate whether or not the Stones' hearing Cocker's version led the band to record the song?

A review of the show appeared in the following morning's newspaper the *Sheffield Telegraph,* headlined "Rhythm And Blues Sheffield City Hall". The reviewer, "F.W." commented,

"A complete cross section of the present popular music phenomena is a difficult thing to find. Last night's concert at the Sheffield City Hall, however, managed this where many others have failed.

The show, rather misleadingly titled the Four Cities Rhythm and Blues Show was presented by the Sheffield brothers Geoff and Pete Stringfellow – and Sheffield groups predominated.

But Rhythm and Blues? Not quite. What was heard was the diluted, terribly English conversion of an essentially Negro culture.

Judged in its own right, however, it was one of the most entertaining and value for money shows ever seen in Sheffield.

The bill toppers, the Rolling Stones and Wayne Fontana and the Mindbenders, are too well known to require much description.

But it was a 19-year-old Sheffield boy, Vance Arnold, who provided for this reviewer the highlight of the evening.

He tackled two extremely difficult numbers, Arthur Alexander's *You'd Better Move On* and *Georgia On My Mind* by Ray Charles, with a feeling and style that would be difficult to find anywhere.

His entire act was well balanced, and his supporting group, the Avengers, did their job competently and without fuss. He is surely a star of the future.

The Four Plus One, the Vantennas, Johnny Tempest and the Cadillacs, Karen Young and the group aptly named the Sheffields all combined to prove that the city is a good second to Liverpool for rhythm and taste in popular music.

It is doubtful whether even Liverpool can offer a better singer in his class than Vance Arnold."

The Rolling Stones – "too well known to require much description"? they'd had one Top 30 hit…and there was no description!

Sixteen years old Julia Taylor (nee Barrett) recollects seeing the show at the City Hall, "They performed *Come On* and I was impressed – they were different! I thought these lads are going to be big. They have a sound of their own. We were able to listen to them ok. There was no screaming as they were relatively unknown at the time." (*You Had To Be There The Rolling Stones Live 1962-69*, Richard Houghton, Gottahavebooks,2015).

In Joe Cocker's biography it was reported that backstage Cocker had met up with his group and his girlfriend Eileen Webster, and the latter "made a beeline for the Rolling Stones, much to his (Joe Cocker's) embarrassment. "She walked up to Mick Jagger and she said, "You're rubbish!" I said "Leave him alone" but she said, "No I'm gonna tell him, he's rubbish. "And I'm saying, "Let the man alone." I always remember she said to him, "You're a big head, you!"" (*Joe Cocker The Authorised Biography*, J P Bean, Virgin Books, 2003).

Interestingly, during September 1963 a handbill produced for shows taking place in October and November at the Stringfellows clubs had The Rolling Stones advertised as performing on November 17th at the City Hall, with local recording star Dave Berry and the Cruisers one of the support acts. In the event the show took place on November 13th without Dave Berry and the Cruisers.

In talking with Dave Berry, he could not recollect the reasons for the show originally advertised for November 17th not taking place.

And a postscript to the show - or rather the poster for the show. There are facsimiles of the poster for the show available for sale – except it's not the authentic poster. Matt Lee, from Sheffield, who has the most extensive memorabilia collection of The Rolling Stones, pointed out that the authentic poster does not have the year of the show identified on it. A look at the made-up poster and the year is there – and in a different size typeface to the date of the show.

Matt Lee's book has the authentic poster and very much more besides (*Hot Stuff The Story Of The Rolling Stones Through The Ultimate Memorabilia Collection*, Welbeck, 2021).

The next date on the tour was in two days' time at the Coop Ballroom Nuneaton - a matinee and evening performance.

The Rolling Stones' second single, *I Wanna Be Your Man*, released on 1st November 1963 reached number 12 in the charts and stayed there for 16 weeks.

And the main item reported locally on the day of the show? The front-page headline in *The Star* – "Police Chief Not Resigning, Says Solicitor".

The article highlighted, Mr Kenneth Mitchell (Solicitor), who "…said there was no question of the Chief Constable resigning…Mr E.V. Staines (Chief Constable) "is absolutely confident that he will be back at his job as head of the police as soon as this matter is sorted out…."

Meanwhile the article noted that the MP, "Sir Gerald Nabarro is on Monday to ask the Attorney General "what proposals he has for initiating prosecutions in connection with the City of Sheffield Police abuses.""

The Chief Constable, Mr E.V. Staines resigned a week later on 20th November 1963.

Chapter 4

Thursday 27th February 1964

City Hall

Two Shows – 6.20pm and 8.50pm

By Arrangement with Stigwood Associates Arthur Kimbrell presents….

All Stars '64

The Rolling Stones billed as "Special Guest Stars", with John Leyton as top billing supported by The Swinging Blue Jeans, Mike Sarne, Don "Fireball" Spencer, Billy Boyle, Mike Berry, Billie Davis, Jet Harris and Bern Elliott & The Fenmen."

The running order of the show – Billy Boyle, Compere – Don "Fireball" Spencer, Billie Davis, Mike Sarne, Interval, Jet Harris, The Rolling Stones, Mike Berry and the Innocents, John Leyton.

At the time the *New Musical Express* referred to the Rolling Stones as a "cavemen-like quintet".

The tour began on 31 January 1964 at the Public Hall, Preston and finished on 7 March 1964 at the Winter Gardens, Morecambe - 29 venues in 29 days, two shows a night. Again, the travel to almost all the venues done by van.

Income from the tour for The Rolling Stones reported at £142 for each show.

The Stones' set list – *"Not Fade Away", "Talkin' About You", "Road Runner", "Come On", "Roll Over Beethoven", "Walkin' The Dog", "You Better Move On", "I Wanna Be Your Man"* – with *"Route 66"* and *"Off The Hook"* being substituted at some shows on the tour.

Evidently as the tour progressed John Leyton had to give up the headliner spot because the Stones had become so popular with the release of *I Wanna Be Your Man* and *Not Fade Away*.

Mick Jagger commented that John Leyton was very gracious about his demotion in the billing.

At the City Hall tickets were available on the Platform at 3s. 6d, at 4s. 0d and 5s. 0d on the Balcony, with Circle and Stalls tickets available at 6s. 0d, 7s. 6d, 8s. 6d and 10s. 6d.

As a comparator of prices - entry for top flight football at both Sheffield clubs – Wednesday and United – could be had for 2s. 0d (Adults) and 1s. 0d (Boys) on the terraces with seat prices starting at 7s. 6d.

And in 1964 a pint of milk would cost you 9d, a pint of beer 2s. 3d, 1lb of Walls pork sausages 3s. 4d, a new Ford Cortina car £624 and the average price of a house was £3,092.

Tickets for the concert could be purchased at the music shop Wilson Peck Ltd on Leopold Street Sheffield 1. Postal booking available with an SAE (Stamped Addressed Envelope).

Coinciding with their appearance at the City Hall, *Record Mirror* had a "4 Page Special" under the headline, "The Fabulous Stones" – focussing on their background, their formation and their successes to date. Interesting to note that a quarter page advert in this supplement had a photo of Brian Jones playing the harmonica with the text, "Brian Jones of the Rolling Stones prefers to play a Hohner harmonica. He uses an Echo Super Vamper model 1820 obtainable from all music shops at 10/9" (53p)."

Two weeks prior to the Stones' show in Sheffield *The Star* had an article headlined, "It Couldn't Happen Here Could It..." – written by John Fearnley, with accompanying photos of screaming girls and Adolf

Hitler! The focus of the article on "Beatlemania" and its impact - albeit in the months to come The Rolling Stones would soon be attracting the level of hysteria that had attached itself to the appearances of The Beatles.

Fearnley observed, "It is after the stamping and the squealing have subsided…(it) is less easy to detect an indication of a sense of responsibility. Can this kind of ballyhoo be kept in check? Can it be confined to the kind of channels for which it has been intended?

Before the war it used to be a matter of wonder in this country that Hitler could fill the arenas merely to let off a lot of hot air about the purity of his intentions.

"It wouldn't happen here," we used to say. And we used to look with some kind of amused detachment at Hitler's Wondervogel, which brought young people together in a kind of uniform and with a common purpose.

Again, we said: "That couldn't happen in Britain." Can't it? Hasn't it?

…a disconcerting truth: that group hysteria can be induced here, In this foggy island where we are supposed to be individualists." (*The Star*, February 11 1964).

Fearnley's article opened with: "When the sociologists get round to the task of writing an objective survey of the 1960s…."

And that reminded me - ten years later at university I "tried" Sociology (for one year only) - "Charisma", in sociological terms, was the subject of an hour's lecture.

Something like 100 students gathered in the largest lecture theatre on campus – the cocksure lecturer asking his youthful audience, "Who can give me an example of someone with charisma?"

Silence enveloped the large hall. Having thought about it, my hand went up, called to respond and punctuating the silence I ventured – "Mick Jagger".

"Mick Jagger?" came the retort from the lecturer in a manner that blended astonishment and disbelief. He continued, "You'll be saying Jimmy Saville next".

I wouldn't and I didn't. The brutal swatting away of my suggestion did little for my understanding and interest in Sociology.

Suffice to say I stand by my answer now as I did then.

Back to the City Hall and no less than four package shows took place at the venue in little more than a two-week period – The Rolling Stones, with the three other shows' headliners – Freddie and The Dreamers, Bobby Vee and Billy J. Kramer and the Dakotas.

Underlining that a number of artists performed in different package shows – The Swinging Blue Jeans appeared at the City Hall with The Rolling Stones on Thursday 27th February and back again the following Tuesday with Billy J. Kramer and The Dakotas.

The price of tickets for all four package shows the same.

Only for Acker Bilk and his Paramount Jazz Band on 22nd February were the price of tickets lower – a top price of 7s. 0d.

At the other end of the scale on ticket prices it was the appearance of established international stars, Ella Fitzgerald and the Oscar Peterson Trio a month later on 26th March that attracted premium ticket prices at the City Hall – top price of 20/- (20s. 0d - £1) in the Circle and Stalls.

As for The Rolling Stones and this show, Paul Kington, a Sheffielder, remembers going to the City Hall as a teenager. Looking back, he commented, "Unbelievably I went with my mother who got the tickets!! My father loved the Shadows and Beatles, but I think the Stones were one step too much for him."

On the show he recollects, "It was loud and girls screamed – I remember Jagger and Jones with their long hair, Jagger jumping around and Jones prominent. They played their recently released single *Not Fade Away*.

They remain my favourite group."

The next date on the tour was the following night at Sophia Gardens, Cardiff.

The Rolling Stones' third single, Not Fade Away, released on 21st February 1964, reached number 3 and stayed in the charts for 15 weeks.

Local reporting on the day of the show and the front-page headline of *The Star* – "Bank Rate Up" – noting the "One per cent rise to 5 per cent after stability for a year"; the article explaining it was a "move to steady expansion pace"

And the front page had an article titled "Yeah! Yeah! Yeah!" – the Beatles – using the words from their Number 1 hit, "She Loves You" and commenting, "The Beatles are back...You can see them on TV on Saturday and also read all about them in *Top Stars Special* out the same day."

Inside the newspaper, job adverts were prominent and reflected the times – local firm George Cooper (Sheffield) Ltd were recruiting for a number of positions including "Smart Young Man – Aged 30/40, to take full responsibility of Warehouse, Packing and Despatch."

Chapter 5

29 May 1964

City Hall

2 Shows – 6.20pm and 8.50pm

John Smith Presents…..

The Rolling Stones headlining supported by The Overlanders, David John and The Mood, Julie Grant, The Cyclones, The Barron Knights featuring Duke D'mond, Peter and Gordon and compered by Tony Marsh.

The show was part of their British tour which started on 15 March 1964 at the Invicta Ballroom, Chatham and finished at the Empire Pool, Wembley on 31 May 1964. 57 dates in 78 days. Two shows a night.

The band's earnings were increasing - on average over the tour it was reported they earned £324 per night.

For the City Hall shows tickets were available at 10s. 6d, 8s. 6d, 7s. 6d in the Circle, 12s. 6d, 10s. 6d, 8s. 6d, 7s. 6d in the Stalls, 6s. 6d and 5s. 0d in the Balcony. Tickets available from Wilson Peck Ltd. Later that year (November) The Beatles headlined at the City Hall – top price tickets 17s.6d.

Tickets could not have been selling as well as expected for The Rolling Stones because a week before the show a large advert was placed in *The Star* stating "Tickets still available", and even on the day of the show a similar advert stated "Tickets still available 1st House: Circle 10s 6d. Odd ones both houses at all prices."

Alongside the advert for The Rolling Stones at the City Hall – there was one for "Blackpool 1964 Summer Season Attractions" – at the Tower

Circus, Opera House, Winter Gardens and Grand Theatre. Interesting to note at the Winter Gardens Pavilion along with Dick Emery, The Kaye Sisters, Eddie Calvert and Clinton Ford were "Guest Stars for the entire season The Dave Clark Five" – the so-called Tottenham Sound on the Fylde Coast for a summer residency.

For the Stones and the City Hall the set list comprised a range of numbers most of which were covers, the songs played selected from - *Talkin' About You, Poison Ivy, Walkin' The Dog, High Heel Sneakers, You Can Make It If You Try, I'm A Kingbee, Pretty Thing; Cops And Robbers; Jaguar And The Thunderbird, Don't Lie To Me, Roll Over Beethoven, You Better Move On, Road Runner, Route 66, I Just Want To Make Love To You, I'm All Right, Beautiful Delilah, I Wanna Be Your Man, Not Fade Away.*

Andy Thompson, aged 15, recollected the show at the City Hall – "I saw them at the second house…. We were up in the balcony and you couldn't really hear the Stones because of the screaming…the sound quality wasn't always that great. They were doing a lot of stuff off the first album. A lot of rhythm and blues, *Not Fade Away, I Wanna Be Your Man*….The Stones were on for perhaps 45 minutes." (*You Had To Be There! The Rolling Stones Live 1962-69*, Richard Houghton, Gottahavebooks, 2015).

In *The Star* newspaper the following day – the headline on the front page – "Girls with their eyes on the stars" – a photograph of girls standing behind a barrier – captioned, "These girls are just eight of the enthusiastic fans who waited outside the Grand Hotel, Sheffield, hoping to catch a glimpse of their favourite stars, The Rolling Stones…."

The Grand Hotel situated on Leopold Street in the city centre.

Not missing a chance to promote a complementary publication the article went on, "But there is no need to wait and watch if you want to see the stars. National and local groups are featured in the latest *Top Stars Special* out today (4d)."

In the *Sheffield Telegraph* Maureen Cleave expressed her views, "Parents do not like the Rolling Stones. They do not want their sons to grow up like them; they do not want their daughters to marry them. Never have the middle-class virtues of neatness, obedience and punctuality been so conspicuously lacking as they are in the Rolling Stones."

And two days before The Rolling Stones show, *The Star* reported – "City Is A 'Miss' For The Beatles" stating, "Branded as one of the three most dangerous centres for pop stars in Britain, Sheffield will be by-passed by the Beatles on their autumn tour.

Announcing this yesterday promoter Arthur Howes said there were too few facilities to protect stars from excited fans...the other two "danger spots" for pop stars are Bristol and Portsmouth."

Mr. Howes said that in none of the big halls in the three cities was there a suitable safety curtain to haul down in case of trouble."

For his part Keith Richards had a recollection of Sheffield for a different reason – commenting on their roadie Ian Stewart, "The obsession with trains: that's the other thing about him and Brian (Jones). I remember Sheffield, one of the great railway marshalling yards, and also Swindon – Stu and Brian went out there all f*cking day and it was pissing with rain. I mean the really worst of English weather. They came back all covered in crap and going on about 0034 bogeys…." (*Stu*, Will Nash, Out-Take Limited, 2003). And at that time steam trains were predominant on the British Railways network.

The next date on the tour was the following night at the Adelphi Theatre Slough.

The Rolling Stones' debut LP – The Rolling Stones – released on 17th April 1964 reached number 1 and stayed there for 12 consecutive weeks, and stayed in the charts for 51 weeks.

Not Fade Away released on 21st February the most recent single record.

The major story reported locally on the day of the show had a front-page headline, "NCB Pay Offer To Miners Is Rejected" – the miners rejected a National Coal Board offer of rises from 2s 0d (10p) to 7s 6d (37.5p) a week for 270000 day-wage men.

Evidently at the conference meeting on the pay offer there was a split over acceptance and the Yorkshire delegation swung the vote in favour of rejection – the Yorkshire delegates accounted for one fifth of the voting power.

And separately, a tour by The Rolling Stones starting on 5th September 1964 at the Astoria Theatre, Finsbury Park, London and finishing at the Hippodrome, Brighton on 11th October 1964 was announced in July 1964. Sheffield's Gaumont Theatre scheduled for 12th September. But along with dates at Norwich, York, Nottingham and Southend the Sheffield date was cancelled. The reasons for the cancellations are not clear.

Chapter 6

Thursday 11 March 1965

City Hall

Two Shows – 6.20pm and 8.50pm

Eric Easton presents….

A short fourteen-date tour starting on March 5th 1965 at the Regal Theatre Edmonton and finishing on March 18th 1965 at the ABC Theatre Romford. The tour was described as intense, two shows a night over the fourteen days.

The Rolling Stones supported by Dave Berry and the Cruisers, Goldie and the Gingerbreads, The Checkmates, The Konrads, compered by Johnny Ball (father of Zoe Ball) and with Special Guest Stars, The Hollies.

Tickets priced at 12/6, 10/6 in the Circle, 7/6 in the Stalls, 8/6 and 6/6 in the Balcony. Wilson Peck Ltd was the place to purchase tickets.

The running order of the show – Johnny Ball, The Konrads, Dave Berry and the Cruisers, The Hollies, Interval, The Checkmates, Goldie and the Gingerbreads, The Rolling Stones.

The Stones' setlist – *Everybody Needs Somebody To Love, Pain In My Heart, Down The Road Apiece, Time Is On My Side, I'm Alright, Little Red Rooster, Route 66, The Last Time, I'm Moving On.*

The following day's evening newspaper, *The Star,* reported under the headline "Enter The Stones And The Fans Go Wild":

"Security men at the City Hall, Sheffield, certainly earned their pay during last night's Rolling Stones show.

One girl caused a stir when she sneaked out of a side door, back through another door at the side of the stage, and evaded the rugby-type tackles to leap on stage and hug three of The Hollies.

Though a group with a sometimes comical turn, this little interlude showed their humour to be rehearsed, as they played solidly on, without even a flicker of a smile.

But it seemed most of the girls had been saving their energies and attacks for the Stones.

For when the boys came on individually, they went wild.

The girls put Operation Stones into action. A dozen at a time made little sallies from their seats, and heads down run the gauntlet of the guards"

There were problems at the second show - The Rolling Stones played in the Oval Hall of the City Hall building, the much larger of the three venues in the City Hall. The smaller Memorial Hall is part of the same building, having a wall between it and the Oval Hall.

The Star reported under the headline, "Jarring Notes Spoil Concert":

"No sooner had internationally renowned concert pianist, Sergio Varella-Cid, started his recital in the City Hall last night than he was interrupted by screams. They came, not from his 150 strong audience of music lovers from Sheffield University, but from 2000 youngsters watching the Rolling Stones only ten yards away.

Portuguese Sergio gave up all hope of playing Stravinsky and Prokoviev, he would just not have been heard over the neighbouring twanging of guitars.

Instead, he launched into a loud programme of Beethoven and Chopin. Afterwards, 30 years-old Sergio, who had been playing in the Memorial Hall next to the main hall, complained to the students who had organised his concert: "If I had known this was going to happen, I should have asked for another date."

An embarrassed student spokesman admitted: "We knew about the Rolling Stones, but we hoped it wouldn't interfere."

A member of the City Hall staff confirmed that the students had been told that the concerts would clash but they went ahead with their booking. We can't accept any blame."

The *Sheffield Telegraph* picked up the story the following morning noting the "with it" crowd was in the main part of the City Hall:

"Mr Robin King, the student in charge of serious music at the university said:

"Mr Varella-Cid could not concentrate sufficiently to play Prokoviev and Stravinsky. He said they demanded more concentration and they were not particularly loud or serious pieces.

Instead, he played Chopin and a few short encores which didn't demand so much. All the time you could hear screams and general clashing around.

He was a little disappointed, obviously, but he wasn't terribly angry. In fact, he was extremely composed throughout the whole thing.""

By Saturday the story had moved on and the *Sheffield Telegraph* reported the problems with the recital had reached the Rolling Stones. Under the headline, "Rolling Stones apologise for Sheffield fans" it reported:

"The Rolling Stones pop group have apologised for disturbing a recital given by pianist Sergio Varella-Cid at Sheffield City Hall.

The recital organised by Sheffield University Students' Union Music Committee, was disorganised on Thursday night when teenage squeals from the "Stones" concert in the neighbouring hall caused Sergio Varella-Cid to scrap a delicate finale in favour of heavier pieces by Chopin, Scriabin and De Falla.

Mr John Wagstaff, vice-chairman of the music committee, said last night: "They apologised for the disturbance, but said they had no control over the fans who were making the racket. It was the screaming and squealing that so upset the audience and Senor Varella-Cid.

We are not blaming the Rolling Stones, because we couldn't even hear them. It is the fans that are to blame," said Mr. Wagstaff.

"However, I think the City Hall management could have notified us beforehand that they were appearing on the same night as the recital.

We were not notified until 24 hours before the recital."

Chairman of the music committee, Mr Peter Smith apologised last night to the 150 who attended the recital in the Memorial Hall for the "disturbing noises" coming from the next-door main hall.

The committee has now received an assurance from the City Hall management that they will be notified well in advance of "pop" concerts to avoid a clash of performances."

Problems from the show were not contained to the noise generated by the fans.

A report in the following Monday's *The Star* under the headline "Lipstick Slogans To Stay On City Hall" stated:

"Slogans and names scrawled in lipstick and coloured chalk by pop star fans may stay on the walls of Sheffield City Hall for weeks, Mr Frank Gummer, the manager said today.

The writing covers the outside walls in an almost unbroken band and was left by fans who turned up to see a show given by the Rolling Stones and Dave Berry last week.

Mr Gummer said he doubted if his staff of six cleaners would have time this week to wash off "The Rolling Stones are fab," "Kinks", "Dave Berry is fab" – and hundreds more.

The Estates Committee of Sheffield City Council would have to approve any move to call in an outside firm to clean the walls.

It cost the Corporation about £50 to get rid of writing on the walls after the Beatles performed in 1963, said Mr. Gummer.

He said: "If I had my way, I would press gang about a dozen of the people who wrote on the walls into cleaning them up on a Sunday morning, with television news cameras watching them. The publicity would show them up.

I think parents and teachers should teach their children a bit of respect for public buildings.

He said that if the mess were cleaned up now, it might be back again next month when two more pop star shows are to be held.

Coun. Peter Jackson, a member of the Estates Committee, said the writing on the walls was symptomatic of the times.

"It is certainly a matter which will receive my consideration," he added."

My first event at the City Hall took place in November 1967 and I can vouchsafe the external walls still had "The Rolling Stones" scrawled on them

For the show at the City Hall 16 years old Carol Owen and 17 years old Barbara Sykes recollected their experiences at the first house which started at 6.20pm:

"At City Hall they had seats on the stage so we had to sit on the front seats and behave…When we saw the Stones we were sat on the stage. And they'd turn round and sing to you and wave and things…

…There was screaming from the start of the show to the finish. Dad (commissionaire at the City Hall) managed to get us into the dressing room with the Rolling Stones. They were smoking and drinking…They signed autograph books for us. They were friendly enough." (*You Had To Be There! The Rolling Stones Live 1962-69*, Richard Houghton, Gottahavebooks, 2015).

Dave Berry and the Cruisers supported The Rolling Stones on three British tours in the early 1960s including this one in March 1965.

His recollections of The Rolling Stones and touring with them, "We became good mates together when we went on tour…those were riotous times and you couldn't get in or out of the theatres because the kids were all going crazy. Both my band and the Stones were confident performers having so much fun. We travelled alongside each other, stayed in the same hotels, drank together and went to clubs in various towns…" (*Dave Berry All There Is To Know*, Dave Berry with Mike Firth, Heron Publications, 2010).

Interesting to note that The Konrads on the supporting bill had amongst their number David Jones – who later changed his name to David Bowie.

The day following the show at the City Hall it was reported the Archbishop of Canterbury, Dr Ramsey, had commented, "Modern youth, the Stones and such, are something one has to live with and understand."

The author Nik Cohn offered this view of The Rolling Stones – "The thing about them was that, unlike the Beatles, they didn't balance out but niggled, jarred and hardly ever relaxed. At all times there was tension to them."

Less than a week before the City Hall show in Sheffield, Cohn had seen the band at the Liverpool Odeon:

"Charlie Watts played the all-time bombhead drummer, mouth open and jaw sagging, moronic beyond belief, and Bill Wyman stood way out to one side, virtually in the wings, completely isolated, his bass held up vertically in front of his face for protection, and he chewed gum endlessly and his eyes were glazed and he looked just impossibly bored.

Keith Richards wore T-shirts and all the time, he kept winding and unwinding his legs, moving uglily like a crab, and was shut-in, shuffling, the classic fourth-form drop-out. Simply, he spelled Borstal.

Brian Jones had silky yellow hair to his shoulders, exactly like a Silvikrin ad, and he wasn't queer, very much the opposite, but he camped it up like mad, he did the whole feminine thing and, for climax, he'd rush the front of the stage and make to jump off, flouncing and flitting like a gymslip schoolgirl.

And then Mick Jagger: he had lips like bumpers, red and fat and shiny, and they covered his face. He looked like an updated Elvis Presley, in fact, skinny legs and all, and he moved like him, so fast and flash he flickered. When he came on out, he went bang. He'd shake his hair all down in his eyes and he danced like James Brown, he flashed those tarpaulin lips, and grotesque, he was all sex.

He sang but you couldn't hear him for screams, you only got some background blur, the beat, and all you knew was his lips. His lips and his moving legs, bound up in sausage-skin pants. And he was outrageous; he spun himself blind, he smashed himself and he'd turn his back on the audience, jack-knife from the waist, so that his arse stuck straight up in the air, and then he'd shake himself, he'd vibrate like a motor, and he'd reach the hand-mike through his legs at you, he'd push it right in your face. Well, he was obscene, he was excessive. Of course, he was beautiful." (*Awopbopaloobop Alopbambooom*, Nik Cohn, Paladin, 1970).

And aside from being there at the shows, directly experiencing the performances and the audience reaction, probably as good an indication of the mounting frenzy that accompanied the expectation and tension waiting for the band to appear on stage, is heard on the EP (Extended Play) *Got Live If You Want It* released in June 1965 - the opening track a cacophony of loud, frenzied female voices chanting "We Want The Stones" – apparently recorded with microphones hanging over the balcony in Liverpool and Manchester on the tour in March 1965.

Record Mirror commented on the EP, "Just listening makes you feel as though you're actually in a club with the Stones, dancing, listening and sweating."

One member of the audience at the Sheffield City Hall was my cousin Sue – to my eight years old eyes a very sophisticated young teenager who wore fashionable dangling earrings.

I learnt that Sue had been at the show the following Saturday at Grandma's house in Broughton Road, Sheffield 6 – Saturday mornings the time when all my aunties (4) and cousins (10) on my Dad's side of the family gathered at the house. Being the only lad amongst four sisters, and also living across the other side of the city, Dad – together with me and my younger brother – were occasional visitors on a Saturday morning. This was such an occasion.

I recollect the conversation went something like this – Grandma starting with:

"So, you went to see The Rolling Stones our Sue?"

"Yes, that's right".

"What were they like?"

"They were brilliant"

Grandma's face broke into a smile. A smile looking back that it would be fair to say was an indulgent smile. I'd never heard of the word indulgent at that time but have little doubt it aptly described Grandma's reaction.

Many years later I asked Auntie Brenda (Grandma's youngest daughter) about Grandma's musical interests and favourite artists – "Mantovani and his Magic Strings one of her favourites". Mantovani and The Rolling Stones. A world of difference.

And it's interesting to note for me that Dad had not the slightest reaction and made no comment about The Rolling Stones – his niece could say they were brilliant without any riposte. I suspect given Grandma's comments he was not going to risk any adverse comments from his Ma by letting on to his own views about The Rolling Stones!

In the course of writing this book I asked Sue what she recollected about the show – her main memory is of screaming girls drowning out the show and what a real waste that was.

The next date on the tour was the following night at the Trocadero Theatre, Leicester.

The second album by The Rolling Stones – *The Rolling Stones No. 2* – released on 15th January 1965, it reached number 1 and stayed there for 10 consecutive weeks, with 37 weeks overall in the chart.

The Rolling Stones' single, *The Last Time*, released on 26th February 1965, reached number 1 and stayed at that position for 3 weeks, with 13 weeks overall in the chart.

A story making the news on the day of the show – a front page headline in *The Star* with accompanying photos:

"Welcome Home, Boys" the newspaper reporting, "Who says The Beatles are on the wane? Those who do should have been at London Airport early today when the fabulous four stepped off a plane from the Bahamas where they had been making a film.

Two hundred screaming fans armed with banners, proclaiming: "It's great to have you back," watched their arrival.""

The main headline on the front page – "Kelvin – A Test Case" with the sub-heading "Future of coal depends on city". The report started:

"The future of Britain's whole coal industry will be heavily influenced by decisions taken in Sheffield in the near future", Coal Board chairman Lord Robens said today.

Speaking about the recent rows over the first choice of oil in preference to coal for heating the Kelvin Flats scheme and the new Sheffield Teaching Hospital, Lord Robens said: "Sheffield is a symbol. If coal cannot succeed there, it will be a bad blow to the morale of the whole industry."

Chapter 7

Chat With Dave Berry

Dave Berry and the Cruisers toured as part of a package tour with The Rolling Stones and other artists on three separate occasions in the early 1960s – including the tour in early 1965 and the shows at Sheffield City Hall on March 11th 1965.

Dave Berry's publicist at the time was Andrew Loog Oldham, the manager of the Rolling Stones.

Our chat covered a range of subjects and provides illuminating insights. As Dave recollected,

"The package tours were in their infancy in the early 1960s – they were really more like variety shows.

Many of the tour promoters were "old school" – having promoted the bands of the 1950s, Ted Heath and his Orchestra and other established stars. They may well have thought - maybe hoped – that these youngsters and their new music were a passing fad. The passing fad is still going strong for some of the artists more than 60 years later.

It was the established stars – players in the orchestras who had their world changed, almost overnight.

In the early 1960s the package tours were primitive. No one had experience of these kind of shows. There was a linkman – a compere for the shows – between the acts coming on stage. At the City Hall shows Johnny Ball – the father of BBC Radio's Zoe Ball – was the compere. The audience were keen to see the acts on stage so the compere was not always well received – from time-to-time various things were thrown at them to encourage them to finish and get off stage.

The sound equipment on stage was shared by all the artists. It had to be given the number of artists coming on and going off stage.

There were screaming girls at all the shows which reflected the times.

The Rolling Stones were more a "laddy band" – yes with screaming girls in the audience, while appealing more to young lads than some of the other bands.

I got on well with all the Rolling Stones including their roadie Ian Stewart – and in particular with Bill Wyman. Perhaps Mick Jagger and Keith Richards were a little "standoffish", Charlie was Charlie and didn't say a lot and in those early days Brian Jones was very quiet – maybe because he'd started the band and his position was no longer leader.

I remember one time being backstage on the Everly Brothers, Bo Diddley, Little Richard tour - and Little Richard announcing his entrance to one and all as he came through the door, with his "Well Aawwwright". Great memories.

And there was no hierarchy amongst the bands on tour – everyone was thrown in the mix. All the artists spent time together - going to clubs in towns – where there were clubs, drinking together and going to restaurants. A dress code was in place in the early 1960s for some of those venues – if you weren't wearing the right gear you weren't let in! I remember in Chesterfield I wasn't let in because I was wearing jeans.

Travel to the venues on the tour was done individually by the artists. We stayed in the same hotels - in Sheffield that was at the Grand Hotel on Leopold Street.

All the bands had their own roadie and there was no security for the artists – that came later.

The Stones were starting to make it big by 1965 and I thought at the time there was something about them as performers and musicians that made them stand out – I'm not at all surprised by their success and their longevity."

Our chat took place in March 2023 – and it was good to hear that Dave was going on tour later in the year.

Chapter 8

Monday October 11 1965

Gaumont Theatre

Two Shows – 6.30pm and 8.50pm

Eric Easton Presents….

A 24 dates' tour starting at the Astoria Theatre, Finsbury Park in London on 24th September and finishing at the Granada Theatre in Tooting, London on 17th October. Support artists – Unit Four + 2, Checkmates, Spencer Davis Group, Charles Dickens and the Habits, and The End, compered by Ray Cameron.

Underlining the nature of touring in 1965, photographer Gered Mankowitz commented, "Stu (Ian Stewart the roadie) was the one who had to try to get everybody together, as he was the only roadie. There was nobody helping him with the kit; it was terribly primitive. The Stones travelled in those days with Charlie's drums, the boys' guitars, a little VOX keyboard. There was no PA, no lights and no monitors…Stu would just lug all the stuff out. And he'd do it all." (*Stu*, Will Nash, Out-Take Limited, 2003).

For the show at the Sheffield Gaumont an advert in *The Star* three nights before their appearance stated, "A few of most seats available" – in most of the price categories. Tickets had not been selling like the proverbial hotcakes.

On the day of the show the front page of *The Star* with the headline "60 men on guard in "Stones" theatre tonight". Alongside a photo of the group it reported, "A Guard of 60 men will be stationed in the Gaumont Cinema, Sheffield, tonight, when the Rolling Stones appear.

The appearance is part of their controversial national tour.

This weekend, 70 local rugby players had to be drafted into the Odeon Leeds to keep order. And 24 hours earlier Mick Jagger was cut about the forehead when an object was thrown at him from among the audience in Stockton."

Gaumont manager Harry Murray is bringing in 22 security men and over 23 casuals to supplement the regular staff.

They will be posted about the theatre and immediately outside to prevent "gate-crashers."

External security arrangements are being left to Sheffield City Police, who declined to say today what arrangements they had in place.

"We will deal with the situation as it occurs," commented a police spokesman.

Said Mr. Murray: "It is quite an operation. We are taking new precautions not so much to protect the Rolling Stones, as our patrons. We do not want people trampling about and hurting each other."

The Stones setlist for the show – *She Said Yeah, Mercy Mercy, Cry To Me, The Last Time, That's How Strong My Love Is, I'm Moving On, Talkin' About You, Oh Baby, (I Can't Get No) Satisfaction.*

In *The Star* the following day there was no doubt about how the performances had been received. Under the headline, "Rolling Stones Fans Get Plenty Of Satisfaction", it reported:

"The Rolling Stones stage show at the Gaumont Cinema, Sheffield, last night, lived up to expectations by being very loud – and extremely popular.

If not technically perfect, the overall sound of the group was powerful – which was just what the audience wanted.

As the show progressed the screams gradually built up, culminating in an ear shattering welcome for the Stones.

Mick Jagger's vocals were, for the main, indecipherable but the Stones material was just recognisable thanks to the over-powering backing of the rest of the group.

Their leader cavorted and danced around the stage, manipulating his stand mike and making up for the lack of audibility with his astounding visual appeal.

Closing the first half of the show, Unit Four Plus Two were equally lacking in vocal coherency despite two singers.

The Checkmates and the Spencer Davis group were both well received as were Charles Dickens and the Habits.

Variety was lacking in the show. The supporting acts all sounded very much alike despite their differing sounds on record.

This was the Rolling Stones' night, however, and the other groups merely served as time-fillers. As the Stones were announced the screams began in earnest and continued until the final curtain.

The Stones closed the show with a lengthy version of their latest hit record *I Can't Get No Satisfaction* – a little incongruous as the fans were obviously well-satisfied."

The newspaper's front-page report ended with a question – "What happened to the riots?" – the reader invited to turn to Len Doherty's story inside the newspaper. And fascinating it is too.

Taking up most of page 5 it headlined, "Len Doherty takes a searching look at the ...Night The Rolling Stones Had A Quiet Time". The article reads:

"In Dusseldorf, riot police used motorcycles and hoses to drive back mobs; in Belfast, car roofs were buckled and windows smashed; in Glasgow, mounted police were needed.

But in Sheffield the modern version of Gilbert and Sullivan or Ivor Novello came and went with never a broken pane or fractured bone.

The riot-raisers "didn't get no satisfaction" out of last night's visit by the Rolling Stones to the Gaumont.

Well, that's showbusiness for you – or to be more precise, that's Sheffield for you. Both inside and outside the theatre the security arrangements were so tight that unruly behaviour was nipped before it even budded. And the kids had more important things to do than stage riots.

There were the usual shrieking-crying-fainting scenes, but the casualties were whipped out of their seats, revived, and back to enjoy more in less time than it takes to write on a wall: "Mick Jagger is fab…"

And it would be easier to break into Fort Knox with Goldfinger than it was to gatecrash the security arrangements at the theatre.

Manager Harry Murray who has seen it all in his 37 years of showbusiness kept his arrangements a strict secret, but handled the whole thing as though it were a state visit by an unpopular dictator.

"Once the Stones began their tour in this country, I started keeping tabs on what happened each place they appeared and worked out a pattern," Harry said.

"Obviously, the answer was not to let the rioting even look like starting, and it was just a matter of finding the best way." The battle plans were worked out in a 10-hour stretch.

Handling teenagers suffering from self-induced hysteria is, Harry believes, a matter of approach: "You can create the right atmosphere yourself. Don't push the kids about and don't go up to them as though they were anything but nice people – customers who paid for their seats. I make the arrangements and then resist any temptation to go dashing about setting people's nerves on edge."

Inside the cinema were 72 security men, including 13 managers or assistant managers from other cinemas in the group. The rest had been hired for the evening. They lined the aisles and formed a human barrier in front of the stage, looking as blandly benevolent as Godfathers at a mass christening.

But when a camera flashed it was immediately removed until the end of the show, when girls collapsed they were immediately carried out past their oblivious best friends, and when over-enthusiastic worshippers tried climbing on the shoulders of those in front, waving their "Mick, I am yours," slogans, they were seated firmly and fast.

The police were in strength outside when the Husky (motor vehicle), which had picked up the Stones at Manchester Road arrived: while a falsetto chorus of fans waited at the front, the all too casually dressed quintet arrived at a side door.

A group of large policemen over-awed the forlorn looking group of little girls who piped a few squeaky pledges of undying adoration and quickly subsided.

"After all," Harry Murray said, "It's all pretty harmless so long as it doesn't get out of hand, isn't it?...The kids get a lot of energy out of themselves and go home tired out and happy."

They certainly looked tired out at the end of each show, but faces were wet with tears, mouths hung slack and nerveless and a general pallor and lassitude covered the youngsters as they floated off home about three feet above the pavements. There must have been some red-eyed classes in Sheffield schools this morning.

Inside the hall they'd used up every ounce of energy enjoying the show without hearing one word of any song. The booming and the twanging and mouth organ wails came through the screaming, but the singers of each group cavorted around the stage soundlessly jitterbugging with their metal microphones.

Was it because they knew they couldn't be heard and they went in for contortionism on the stage I asked Mr. Jagger. No, no, they like to give it everything they've got. Which is quite a lot of calories in energy.

To me the group looked tired off-stage, smaller and frailer than television makes them. But no, they said, they were enjoying the tour despite the fact that this was the quietest appearance so far – and the hall was rocking when they said it.

Why then, apart from the security arrangements, did Sheffield take them so quietly?

"We're here often, that's why," said the agile Mr. Jagger. "We were only here in April – they're used to us."

He also felt the average age of audiences in Sheffield was older than in many places: "For every youngster out there you see a grown-up. They're quieter…"

I did see a couple of Mums, but apart from them even two 21-year-old nurses looked like grandmothers compared to the average shrieker. Yet even at their early age the girls had the technique of ruckus-raising well worked out.

One girl tries a couple of tentative "eeks" like a sparrow seeing if anyone's home. Someone else matches it with a louder "ooh" and the harmony is tossed backwards and forwards from seat to seat.

Then it's every girl for herself, and by the time Mr. Jagger was doing a tasteful strip-tease involving taking off his jacket and unbuttoning, but not rolling up, his sleeves, they would have screamed their heads off at Sir John Barbirolli singing *Lover Come Back To Me.*

In the meantime, the boys sit in small pools of silence with stony faces unable to hear the singers, showered with sweets meant for the stage and wishing they'd got a guitar.

Far from looking like potential rioters, the girls looked like little mermaids hopelessly and sexlessly calling out to passing sailors who can't even hear them. At the end of the second show the Stones were whipping off the stage into a car and off towards Doncaster while the audience still waited hopefully for a third curtain call.

Momentarily disappointed, emotionally exhausted and with electronic acoustics still booming in their heads, they all trooped off peacefully home. The policemen outside dispersed and the 72 security men inside took the cotton wool out of their ears.

"And yet with the wrong handling it could have been just the opposite," said Mr. Murray, whose security didn't prevent him from taking pity on a couple of kids who had lost their tickets but stopped looking utterly devastated when they were slipped into spare seats. "Riots are easily started if an adult does the wrong thing."

The youngsters had eaten 600 hot dogs, 2000 ices, bought 1000 programmes and 1000 copies of the magazine *Showtime.*

"Oh yes, they spend," said Harry. "It's a night out they'll remember for months. And that's what we have to remember when they get lively.

Treat them with a bit of tenderness isn't as soft a slogan as it sounds. It means a lot to the kid to be given the VIP treatment on a night like this."

And with all the shrewdness of the life-long showman he grinned and added:

"BESIDES. THEY'RE THE GROWN-UP CUSTOMERS OF A FEW YEARS FROM NOW WHO'LL BE COMING HERE AND TELLING ME THEY DON'T UNDERSTAND WHAT KIDS NOWADAYS SEE IN POP GROUPS…."""

(The last paragraph in upper case as reproduced in the newspaper report).

One of the extra security men that night at the Gaumont Theatre – my Dad.

As an ex-serviceman he had become a member of the Corps of Commissionaires and the job had come through from the Corps regional headquarters in Leeds. He'd been pleased to accept the job and whatever his views on The Rolling Stones – negative that they were – he was not going to turn down the opportunity to earn extra money (his full-time job at this time - a steelworker in the Sheffield and Hallamshire steelworks).

His recollections of the evening - loud, incessant screaming. And with many screaming, teenage girls taking their chance to run down the aisleway shouting "Mick, Mick…." And then collapsing into the arms of the waiting security men who quickly moved them away from the stage, and to the back of the auditorium. No sooner had one girl been carried away than another teenage girl came screaming down the aisle – the operation was on repeat many times over.

In truth Dad could not understand what possessed girls to act and behave in this way.

His other main recollection of his duties that evening was being briefed before the show - the security men (and they were all men) were to be lined up at the back of the theatre as The Rolling Stones came on stage, and at a given signal from the security manager they would all make for the front of the stage facing the audience.

It was inevitable that the hurried marching of the phalanx of security men came early in the show….Dad arrived at the front of the stage and initially facing the lead singer he was confronted by Mick Jagger swivelling on his axis, bending over and sticking his backside in the air directly in front of him. Not a sight that endeared Mick to Dad. Nor did the purple trousers Mick was wearing appeal to his sartorial taste.

And drummer Charlie Watts had cause to remember the Gaumont shows - in a *Tiger Beat* magazine interview he observed, "A huge stage and the only way up through a kinda footballers' tunnel in the middle. I'm sitting there peacefully bashing away on *The Last Time* when this well-dressed geezer comes up the tunnel and starts whispering urgently in my earhole. I thought he has the manager tipping us off that there was to be a police raid. He wants my autograph! How daft can you get? Have you ever heard of a three-armed drummer? Still bashing away, I tell him to wait. Next moment he pulls me off my stool and I'm dumped on the floor with all the gear on top of me. And he's still insisting on an autograph!"

A fan's recollection of the show – Andy Thompson Aged 16 – "I remember Unit Four + 2 were on with them, and maybe the Nashville Teens. At that time Jagger was wearing the sweatshirt with horizontal lines on. I remember them doing "Johnny was a rockin" (*Around and Around*). Brian Jones wore a white polo neck sweater. The screaming was slightly toned down compared with 1964. You could actually hear them." (*The Rolling Stones in the Sixties A People's History,* Richard Houghton, Spenwood Books, 2022).

As for the lead singer, things could be problematic on stage – three days earlier at the ABC Theatre in Stockton, Mick Jagger had been hit by a coin thrown by a fan – and pictured with a plaster below his left eye, he commented, "My eye has gone through all the colours of the rainbow during the past few days. But it's almost cleared up now." (*Disc Weekly*, 23 October 1965).

The mass hysteria of teenage girls in the first half of the 1960s - with the Beatles and the Rolling Stones - is a phenomenon in itself. Nik Cohn after the show in Liverpool went back to the auditorium and observed, "…there was this weird smell. Piss: the small girls had screamed too hard and wet themselves. Not just one or two of them but many, so that the floor was sodden and the stench was overwhelming". (*Awapbopaloobop Alopbamboom*, Paladin, 1970).

In the week of the show at the Sheffield Gaumont Mick Jagger was quoted in *Disc Weekly* magazine – the article opened, "Sitting in bed in a Northern Hotel (possibly the Hallam Tower Hotel in Sheffield), nursing a bad cold this week, Mick Jagger told me a little of the Stones' attitude to their fans.

"I don't get worried when girls get on stage and throw themselves at me," he said. "Only last night a very heavily built girl made the stage and actually floored me.

"It's not the ones that get on stage who get hurt. It's the ones that don't make it and get trapped in the orchestra pit that usually get clobbered. We had to throw a guy out the other night for hitting the fans. He was employed to stop them getting on stage.

"Why should a 12 years old girl get thrown out of a theatre just for standing up and screaming a bit? That girl has probably saved for weeks to buy her twelve-and-six ticket and then gets kicked out after seeing two minutes of our act."

On the broader point of the contagion of mass hysteria – within a venue, across the country, across the world - The Beatles and Beatlemania its first manifestation in this country in the early 1960s…and then hysteria for The Rolling Stones. I was too young to attend any of the Sheffield shows in the 1960s.

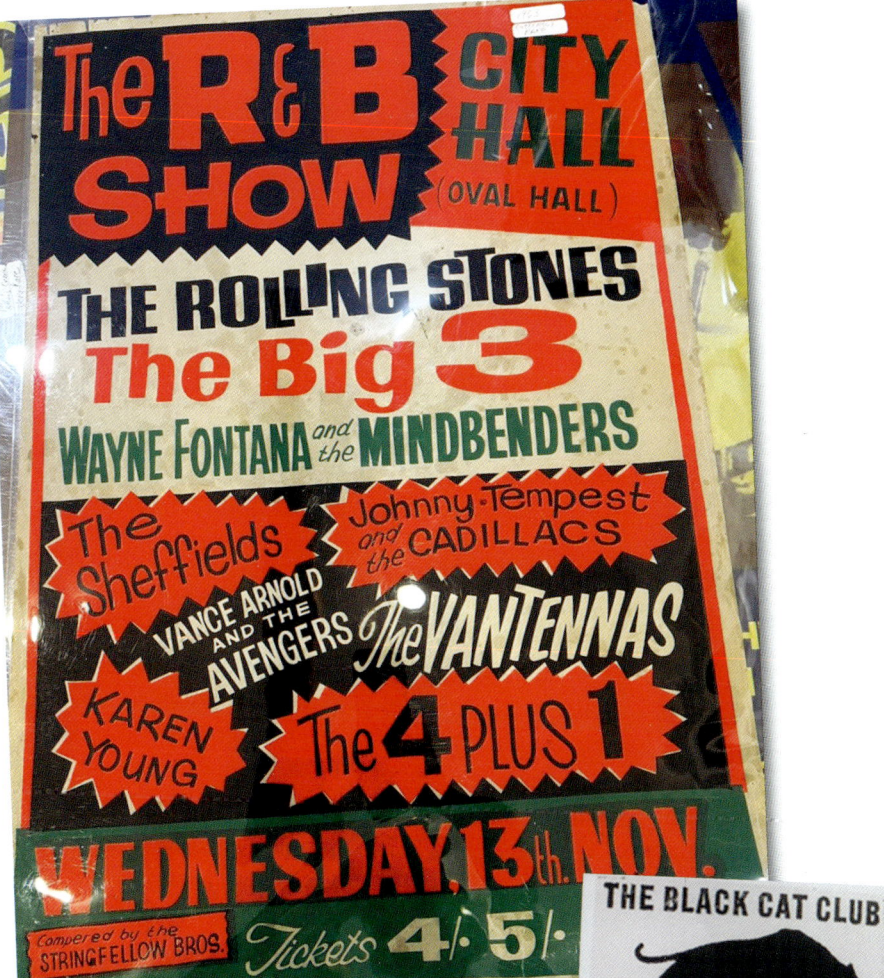

Authentic poster for the
November 13th 1963 show
at the City Hall.
(Courtesy of Matt Lee)

Poster for the show that never was.

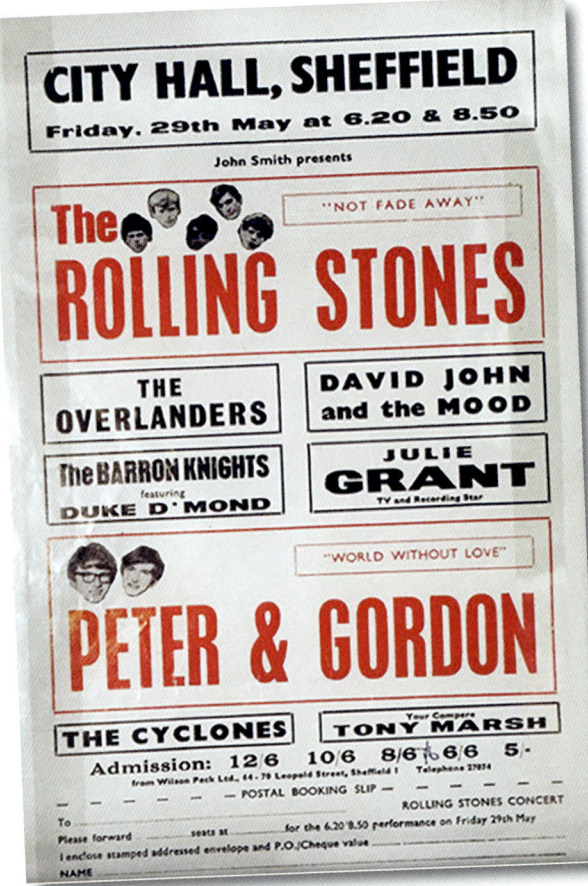

Girls waiting for the Stones outside the Grand Hotel Leopold Street, February 27th 1964 *(Courtesy of Sheffield Newspapers)*

Poster with booking slip for the 29th May 1964 concert at the Sheffield City Hall

Article in The Star - Len Doherty backstage with the Stones after the two Gaumont shows 11th October 1965
(Courtesy of Sheffield Newspapers)

Fans in front of the stage at the Don Valley Stadium 9th July 1995
(Courtesy of Sheffield Newspapers)

Mick Jagger on stage at the Don Valley Stadium July 9th 1995
(Courtesy of Alamy)

The Rolling Stones on stage - Ronnie Wood, Mick Jagger, Keith Richards....Darryl Jones in the background - at the Don Valley Stadium 6th June 1999 *(Courtesy of Alamy)*

Mick Jagger on the video screen looks out over the band playing on stage at the Don Valley Stadium 27th August 2006 *(Courtesy of National World)*

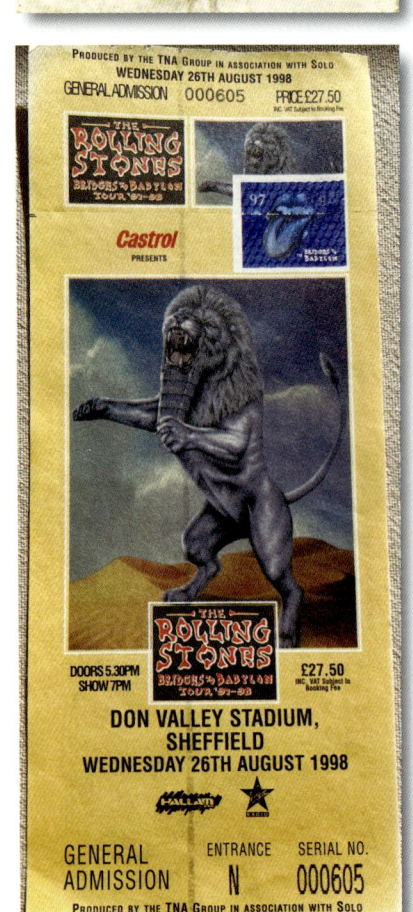

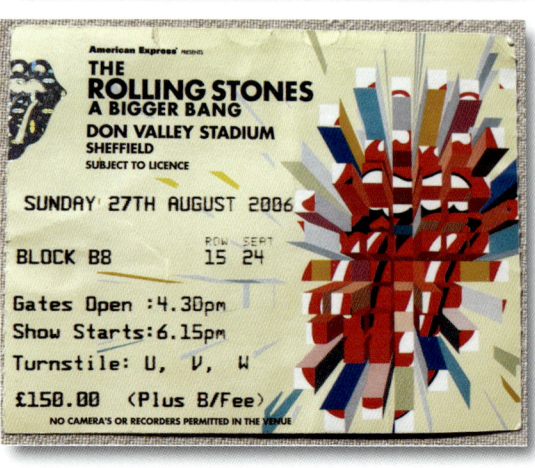

Tickets for The Rolling Stones shows in Sheffield

We'd heard on the news about screaming girls at shows for The Beatles and The Rolling Stones – we'd not witnessed it first-hand.

That is with one exception - a screening of the Beatles' film "A Hard Day's Night" at the Gaumont in late 1964. I went to see the film with a group of friends. The moment the first Beatle appeared on the film – screaming, loud screaming – from at least two girls in the audience. Utterly unnerving and completely bonkers. It's celluloid, two dimensional. Thankfully the screamers ceased after a minute of disturbing everyone else in the cinema. If that's how they react to a film it took little imagination to picture reactions at a live show

On the logistics for the autumn 1965 tour Bill Wyman observed, "Things on this tour were much better organised…. One thing that made it easier for us was the fact that we stayed in hotels that were well away from where we were actually performing." (*Rolling With The Stones*, Dorling Kindersley, 2002). This approach had the consequence of a smaller number of girls clamouring to see the band in their hotel.

In Sheffield the Hallam Tower hotel on Manchester Road provided the base for the band – about 3 miles from the city centre.

The next date on the tour was the following night at the Gaumont Theatre Doncaster.

The Rolling Stones single, *(I Can't Get No) Satisfaction*, released on 20th August 1965, reached number 1 in the charts, and stayed there for 2 weeks, and was in the chart for twelve weeks overall.

For Sheffield Wednesday supporters the tune and rhythm of *Satisfaction* was the basis of a popular terrace chant that season as the team progressed to the FA Cup Final – limited in its usage of words the emphasis being on the song's beat, "Da da da Wednesday da da…." and repeat as many times as desired.

The Rolling Stones LP. *Out Of Our Heads*, released on 4th September 1965, reached number 2 in the chart and stayed there for 24 weeks.

Interesting observations in *Disc Weekly* (October 16th) – on the front page "Jagger names top record reviewer" – *Disc Weekly's* very own Penny Valentine – "She's a good reviewer because when she's finished writing you know something about the record he commented."

Inside that week's edition a letter from Mick Jagger is printed criticising reviewer Nigel Hunter, "After reading your review of our new LP *Out Of Our Heads*, I think you must have an intellectual music complex…You've never given any of our EPs or LPs good reviews. Maybe they're all bad! I personally think the job of a reviewer is to tell the reader a bit about the record as well as giving your views".

Hunter had the right of reply, "I never said I didn't like your LP. I said I couldn't understand what all the fuss was about…I agree reviewers should let readers know something about the records as well as their own opinions, but I'm not nearly as blonde and pretty as Penny, and I don't get as much space. Gee, life's tough, isn't it?"

Locally the main headline on the front page of *The Star* on the night of the show – "Board Wants Soap Price To Be Pegged" – Glen Allan reported, "Good news for housewives today – prices for soap and detergents may be pegged.

And there may be fewer of those soap powder television adverts.

A Prices and Incomes Board report on the soap industry recommends: There should be no price increases either of soap or detergents before the end of next year…."

Chapter 9

Between Times – 1965 – 1995

Between times is a long time – almost 30 years between the last show in Sheffield in 1965 and the next Rolling Stones show at the Don Valley Stadium in July 1995.

Books have been written about The Rolling Stones covering a much shorter period. For the purposes of brevity important events and landmarks are recorded in this chapter.

Personnel changes to the band are to the fore – Brian Jones evidently becoming increasingly unreliable as a result of his drug use parted ways with The Rolling Stones in June 1969; within a month he was found dead in the swimming pool at his house in Sussex.

Welwyn Garden City's Mick Taylor replaced Jones as guitarist and stayed with The Rolling Stones until 1974.

Ron Wood - previously with The Faces – joined the band as Taylor's replacement in 1975.

Bassist Bill Wyman left The Rolling Stones in 1992 replaced on tour by bassist Darryl Jones.

Ian Stewart – often referred to as "the sixth stone" – passed away in 1985. An original band member when The Rolling Stones formed in 1962, he became the roadie for the Stones at their shows in the 1960s.

Their manager changed in 1967 – Andrew Loog Oldham was replaced by the American Allen Klein (who also managed The Beatles post-Brian Epstein's management).

The Rolling Stones reputation grew as the 1960s progressed – both as a band and for their off-stage activities.

The infamous drugs-bust at Redlands, Keith Richards' home in West Sussex in 1967 – resulting in both Richards and Mick Jagger spending time in prison – Wormwood Scrubs in London. *The Times* ran a leader article - "Who Breaks A Butterfly On A Wheel" – essentially focussed on the over-reaction of the judiciary to events in Sussex.

That may well have helped in reducing jail time to a matter of days. But no matter – as many people saw it the Stones had been made scapegoats. For many of the older generation the Stones were having just too good a time, and got what was coming to them.

Aghast at what had befallen the Stones other bands showed their support – The Who making a record in solidarity with The Rolling Stones – covering their songs, *The Last Time* and *Under My Thumb*.

Musically the band achieved their eighth No 1 single before the end of the decade – *Honky Tonk Women*.

A free concert in London's Hyde Park in July 1969 took place little more than a week after Brian Jones' death – 250000 in attendance.

Later that year a free concert at the end of their tour of the United States at the Altamont Speedway in California…..700000 people, policed by Hells Angels. Evidently a number of people in the audience high on drugs. Chaos, disaster, tragedy. A young black man – Meredith Hunter - stabbed to death in front of the stage while the Stones were performing. All of this captured on the Maysles Brothers film, *Gimme Shelter* – advertising for the film highlighted, "the music that thrilled the world…and the killing that stunned it!"

The following year – 1970 – the Stones left Britain. They had no financial choice. Tax. The punitive tax rates applied at the time meant they would have been owing money to the Inland Revenue. The band members and their families decamped to France. All this made headline news with all the attendant national publicity.

The band left Decca Records and set-up their own label, Rolling Stones Records in 1971…but not before fulfilling their contractual obligations to Decca Records by producing a final single – the infamous, *C**ksucker Blues.*

Musically the years between 1968-1972 were arguably the band's most fertile period – a string of classic albums released in succession, *Beggars Banquet, Let It Bleed, Sticky Fingers* and *Exile on Main Street*.

Major tours of the USA and Europe took place in 1972 and 1973, and again in 1975 and 1976.

Fast forward to 1977. Margaret Trudeau – the wife of Premier Pierre Trudeau (mother of Canadian Premier Justin Trudeau) - to all intents and purposes went missing in 1977…the Canadian Premier's wife had gone missing. Missing for days. She surfaced to the full glare of the public spotlight at the Castle Harbour Hotel in Toronto. Other guests at the same hotel? The Rolling Stones. She had been spending time with the band. Mayhem – national headlines, the Canadian dollar fell 10% on the news, worldwide headlines.

Further tours in 1978 (USA), 1981 and 1982 – USA and Europe respectively.

And then a fallow period – no tours, and little new music between 1982-89. Jagger and Richards particularly focussed on solo work.

Back with a bang in 1989 – a major tour of the USA – the themed "Steel Wheels Tour" and the following year in Japan and Europe the "Urban Jungle" tour: a total of 115 shows, grossing a reported $175 million – the most successful rock tour to date. And with massive stage sets on a scale not seen before for The Rolling Stones.

Chapter 10

Sunday 9 July 1995

Don Valley Stadium

Voodoo Lounge

European Tour 95

Volkswagen Presents….

The first show by the Rolling Stones in the Don Valley Stadium – an open-air venue built for the World Student Games hosted by Sheffield in 1991.

The Voodoo Lounge Tour took place during 1994 and 1995 – starting in the USA and visiting Canada, South America, South Africa, Japan, Australia and New Zealand before European dates starting in Amsterdam in May 1995. 129 shows over a 13-months period. The European tour sponsored by carmaker Volkswagen. A reported $320 million grossed for the tour – the highest grossing tour of all time. Revenues now reported in dollars. It was big business.

The Sheffield show kicked-off the British leg of their Voodoo Lounge Tour – 4 shows in this country – Don Valley, 2 shows at Wembley and one at Brixton Academy in London.

Reported attendance for the Sheffield show of 49308.

It was a huge logistical exercise – the whole nature of the shows had changed almost beyond comprehension since the 1960s – no more travelling to the shows in a van, sharing the sound equipment with all the artists on the bill.

There was now a major set design, a major lighting show, sound equipment to ensure tens of thousands of people could hear the show in an outdoor arena, and video screens so that the band could be seen. And add to that a stage that enabled the performers – and the frontman in particular – to use it to the full, including a cordless microphone which enabled free movement for him on stage.

The term lead singer was now nowhere near adequate in describing Mick Jagger on stage. He was the frontman. The frontman in front of tens of thousands of fans. The one who made things happen with the audience – engaging, coaxing, encouraging. The frontman for the show – and it was a show - no more the lead singer at a concert.

The Star played its part in promoting the Rolling Stones arrival in the city after a thirty-year absence.

On July 6th it headlined – "Voodoo Magic" – "The Stones are set to roll into Sheffield – and YOU could be meeting them!" – confirming that it was "the only newspaper in the region to offer the chance for two people to meet the Rolling Stones" – in fact it was for two pairs of tickets. To enter the exclusive competition simply confirm the name of the first single from the current album, *Voodoo Lounge* – entries by postcard. The prize? To meet the individual members of the band and take a guest to the after-show party.

I didn't win!

David Dunn in the "Relax" section of the newspaper commented, "They've thrilled just about every race and creed on earth – this weekend Sheffield becomes the first city in Britain to get a dose of The Rolling Stones 90s style.

The stage is huge – about the width of a football pitch – and nothing short of what you would expect of the pub band who became the originators of stadium rock.

As work on re-constructing the monster begins in earnest at Don Valley Stadium, the facts, figures and reviews confirm it to house one of the greatest shows on Earth."

"Voodoo Facts" are revealed:

- The stage show was transported in 72 ocean containers, three 747 planes and 56 lorries
- It takes 50 people a day (120 on the final day) to erect it
- It features the world's largest mobile video screen
- Forty tons of ballast water (an Olympic swimming pools' worth) beneath the stage
- The futuristic cityscape set cost £3 million
- It uses 3,840,000 watts of power – roughly the daily supply to 4000 homes
- There are 1500 aircraft landing lights built into the stage
- The sound system blasts out more than 40000 home hi-fi's
- A primary feature of the set is the 27 metres long Cobra – an arm like structure climbing upwards with its 48 aircraft landing lights
- The set comprises 600 tons of steel

The newspaper observed, "The band called in set designer Mark Fisher to help turn their wild ideas (about the set) into reality.

"The Stones are fearless and powerful people who will make a statement and stand by it," said Fisher.

There were two major criteria for the Voodoo Lounge set, "That Barbara Streisand shouldn't be able to sing on it, and that Prince Charles shouldn't like it."

The idea was to combine two concepts: the cyberworld of a 21st century super-highway and ancient superstition."

It was a more than impressive set.

I recollect my cousin Julia – a resident of Sheffield - mentioning that she had taken her four-year-old son Keith down to the Don Valley Stadium as the set was being erected. Evidently, they were very impressed by what unfolded before their eyes.

The newspaper quoted band members:

"Once it comes to town it's like a circus going up, people come, then it goes," says Mick Jagger, who even at this point in his career admits to a few butterflies.

"If you're not nervous going on in front of 50000 people you're not functioning.

It's a great moment for me – it's like any event where you get a lot of people, you encourage them to do something where they all feel they're part of the same experience."

Charlie Watts – "Mick is the best entertainer in the world live. To see him work a stage for two hours is something special, and he's got better and better."

On the observation that seven new songs are played in the set, some rare oldies and fans favourites including *Honky Tonk Women* and *Brown Sugar*, Ronnie Wood commented – "There's still the element of the unknown. We love that risk element – making them more raw and earthy and valid. It's not just a repetition of a set list".

Keith Richards added, "All of our songs are tailormade for live and they can grow on stage. And when it comes to playing live the people have got the hottest band in the world."

More facts revealed by *The Star* on the penultimate day before the show – changes at the stadium included:

- Ripping out seating to make three massive new exits
- Converting changing rooms to a medical centre
- Four first aid posts created on the running track area
- Plumbing in 20 standpipes to provide water for the fans
- Covering the grass on the pitch with a protective surface
- Refreshment tents and Merchandising stalls built

Under the headline "Valley of the Kings" – journalist Paul Whitehouse commented, "The Rolling Stones' Sheffield concert will be the country's biggest rock music spectacle of the year. It is rumoured that the band themselves chose Don Valley stadium for their only English concert outside the capital because they approved of the venue's image.

That is a major stamp of approval for the stadium, which has hosted just three other similar shows."

Exactly what the image of the stadium was is not revealed.

Mr. Whitehouse goes on to comment how the eyes of the music business will be focussed on the stadium as a possible venue for other world class acts. "They are determined to make the most of this opportunity and have planned the show down to the last detail. Stadium staff, emergency services, licensing officials and the Stones' promoters have been working on plans since the concert was announced in November."

Stadium safety officer Pat Smith acknowledged there would be inevitably some traffic disruption and commented, "The licence (for the show to go ahead) will be signed by Sheffield City Council's officer only when he is satisfied with all preparations. That may be anything up to one minute before the doors open."

Looked at dispassionately if that last point became reality, it could cause mayhem.

In the *Yorkshire Post* the headline confirmed what was to come, "Stones roll in to stun city with "greatest rock show on earth"".

And this was an open-air venue – the first one The Rolling Stones had played in Sheffield.

I'd seen them play at Wembley Stadium in 1982 and at Manchester City's Maine Road football ground in 1990 as part of the Urban Jungle Tour.

Both open-air venues, and for both shows standing positions for us on the pitch. And I'd picked up a few important pointers from those experiences:

- The earlier you arrive the closer to the stage your position is likely to be
- The earlier you arrive inevitably the longer the wait time for the show...and there's a lot of waiting
- Arrival of The Rolling Stones on stage?....after the support act has finished their set many false alarms as the taped music continues to blare out from the speakers – and then a period of silence - as fans started to feel this must be it, they're on their way...except it wasn't and the taped music started up again.

The best guide I'd worked out to establish when the Stones would appear on stage was the arrival of the guys who operated the lights from their towers facing the stage. Until they arrived and started climbing to their seated cradle near the top of those towers there was no chance of the show starting. Once they're in position – and engaging in a few practice beams of coloured lights to make sure they're working well - we're no more than 10 minutes away from the start of the show.

At this point crowd expectations heighten – there's a rush towards the stage, some – particularly young ladies – are taken by surprise and knocked to one side. Another scramble. The crowd density increases noticeably as people get closer to the stage. Carefully laid out plans by fans arriving early, anticipating their chosen area would be theirs and theirs alone, were shattered as the scramble forward gained momentum.

- Toilets – plentiful but a long way from the standing positions on the pitch
- Merchandising – stalls erected at the venue selling expensive memorabilia – and more annoyingly and frustratingly no queuing system to purchase an item. Simply a scrum of people crowded round the stall – the scrum increasing in size as the evening wore on. And no method by the people selling the goods to determine "who's next?" – other than say those words with the response from everyone within hearing distance of – "me", "over here", "I am". A disorderly scramble would be a kind description – hugely frustrating for the would-be purchaser.

Those experiences at Wembley and Manchester helped in preparation for the Don Valley show:

- We arrived at 6.30pm – gates were open at 5.00pm, far too early for us - we had no idea the time the Stones would take to the stage; £25 unreserved ticket for the pitch
- Merchandise stall first – unsupervised rabble around the stall, pushing to get to the front, eventually served – T-shirt purchased for £20 - still have it - good advert for The Rolling Stones and Castrol the sponsors
- Now toilets – best do that now rather than later – trying to find your way back to a specific place on the pitch was at best problematic and could turn out to be all but impossible.
- Time to find a place on the pitch – it was hot and we'd be more exposed to the heat on the pitch, but better that than being much further away albeit under cover and in a seat. We settled on a little less than half way back quite central, ahead of the Sound Desk…actually just behind Rodger Wylde and his group – Wylde a former Sheffield Wednesday striker of the 1970s. Good taste in music Rodger Wylde.

- Looking at the make-up of the crowd it looked a good mix of men and women, a good cross-section of different ages - from those in their teens to those right through to their sixties.
- Then the wait…..Support band – Del Amitri – came on for their set - they're ok…no more than that …off they go….we're waiting – we're all waiting – for the main men.
- Lighting men ascend the towers….we're on…crowd knows something's up…the taped music stopped…the light fading in Sheffield now
- Crowd expectations rising…this is one of the best parts of a Rolling Stones show for me…the opening, not knowing when they're going to arrive, the theatrics accompanying their entrance and what the opening song will be
- Background noise…instruments…picking up on a song…..pacy, insistent beat…..ah…it's - at that moment the spotlight picks out the frontman as he delivers the opening line to *Not Fade Away*….more lights…the rest of the band now clearly visible on stage…the crowd up for it and rocking….a cornucopia of flashing coloured lights right in front of you…the Cobra breathes out fire and breathes out fire again…and on it goes
- A literal explosion - the senses are pummelled – sight, sound – everything hitting you – tension and anticipation in the crowd released – we're on our way
- And for most of the next two hours eyes are inevitably drawn to Mick Jagger – his movements, his presence, his larger-than-life persona imposed by the video screen, his command of his audience, his showmanship – he demands attention. And my word does he get it.
- First song finished – Keith Richards plays the last guitar note, Charlie Watts the last strikes on his drum and then his cymbals….the crowd respond with climactic applause and acclaim before Watts has made his last note. What a start.

The theatrics were fantastic – took your breath away – the lighting, the fire-breathing cobra, the explosion of noise all top drawer.

The choice of song? – *Not Fade Away* is an old Buddy Holly number – it's not the strongest rocker – but the Stones delivered, Jagger delivered – classic harmonica playing midway through the song, he nailed it. From the opening bars it was "light the blue touch paper" and stand back.

Added to the core band members – Jagger, Richards, Watts and Wood were Darryl Jones on bass guitar (replacing Bill Wyman on tour), a complete brass section, keyboards and vocals support. A long way from the five members of the band on stage at the City Hall and Gaumont.

It may have been thirty years since they last performed in the city but they were back with a bang and a whole lot more.

And it was a great show, a great performance – most of the songs known by the audience, a few less well-known – particularly those from the new *Voodoo Lounge* album.

And it was a performance - perform is the word. In these large outdoor venues – tens of thousands in the audience, huge video screens to transmit the images so that everyone has something to see of the performers. Songs are performed rather than merely played by the musicians – the spectacle is a key and integral ingredient.

At the end of the show there was a state of almost nervous exhaustion – you'd been a part of an experience, and played a full part in it. The audience fed off the Stones and it looked very much like the Stones fed off their audience. Fabulous. As you looked around everyone was visibly enjoying the show and the experience.

Yes, there was an occasional false note – the start to *Satisfaction* was clunky and lacked the crisp notes and pace that only came when the song's mistimed start had been exorcised.

Sparks Will Fly from the new album failed to make a real impact with the audience.

And then you look at all the highs and positives – far too many to recount and list.

My brother and I stayed for the encores – along with the vast majority of the audience – until the final loud acclaim and applause and then the performers were gone. I've no doubt they made it to their resting place for the night a lot quicker than we did. No matter - the show was more than worth it.

And the interaction with the audience during the show? Mick Jagger's verbal engagement with the audience started after the second number – "And welcome Sheffield to the Voodoo Lounge".

He became more expansive after the next song – "Ok. How you doin' out there? We'd like to welcome everyone who has come from out of town. Anyone from Manchester? And from Leeds? Nottingham? Just a few, just a sprinkling."

His observation on "just a few" focussed on those from Nottingham – there were loud cheers in response to Manchester and Leeds.

He went on, "It's been a very, very long time since we've been in Sheffield, indeed it's a very long time since we've been in the north of England. We're really happy to be starting off our gigs in England here."

Given all the other dates were in London he could have asked whether there were people in the audience from Newcastle, Sunderland,

Liverpool, Birmingham and more places besides, and no doubt would have received a positive response.

Before the song *It's All Over Now* he said, "We're gonna do a really old one for you – this is one we played in the ballroom when we played Sheffield many, many years ago. I'm not gonna tell you when". Not sure many people would think of the Gaumont or the City Hall as a ballroom!

And in his band introductions Mick Jagger came finally to the rhythm guitarist stating, "Keith Richards the honky tonk man is going to sing for you."

Keith's response – "That's a threat not a promise."

The guitarist went on, "How you doing Sheffield? How you doing England for Christsakes it's been long enough….they don't let me in much."

And to round off the introductions Ronnie Wood came to the microphone pointing to the frontman with the words – "And a man of steel like yourselves". Huge applause before Mick Jagger temporarily left the stage for the next two numbers.

At the end of the show and before the encore as the band was lapping up the wild acclaim and applause Mick said, "Good night Sheffield…Goodnight….God bless you."

The show was on the front page of *The Star* the following day, with the headline – "The greatest Rock and Roll show on earth We're No 1" The accompanying narrative, "The Godfathers of Rock and Roll took Sheffield by storm last night with the kind of performance that has kept them at the top for over three decades…Don Valley drew an audience comprising original fans, their children, grandchildren and the plain inquisitive".

The front page went on, "Sheffield is today proclaimed as world leader in outdoor pop and rock concerts.

Last night's Rolling Stones gig at Don Valley Stadium went ahead without a single arrest in the 50000 crowd.

Sheffield Council's deputy leader Councillor Peter Price said, "People have always said the stadium was a white elephant – but not anymore.

We were in the international eye and we proved we could do it. People are saying Roundhay Park, Leeds is finished and Manchester is a very poor second.

All the big acts will be looking at Sheffield, we'll certainly be going out to get them. We could have half a dozen next year.""

And the newspaper had this observation from Paul Flower, marketing manager of Midland Concert Promotion, "Europe's biggest gig organisers" – "Don Valley is a brilliant venue. It is the north's equivalent to Wembley.

The show would convince any promoter Sheffield is the premier place to hold outside shows."

South Yorkshire police commented, "There were no reports of any incidents – it was a splendid event and a credit to everybody who was there."

The article concluded, "Their (The Rolling Stones) promises of a massive show – the only date outside London – were kept with one of the most stunning rock events ever staged in the UK."

Inside the newspaper a four page Rolling Stones Special Issue.

The first headline – "In the afternoon sun the unmistakeable whiff of cannabis wafted through the crowd as teachers from Dore (district in Sheffield) sat on the floor eating off flowery paper plates."

An odd headline. For what it's worth we saw no flowery paper plates, certainly the odd whiff of cannabis, we had no idea if teachers from Dore were amongst the crowd.

The article had a more informative comment - "The crowd roared their approval to greet their heroes. By the time darkness fell even the sceptics had been won over by the raw, still rebellious power of the Stones performance."

In a review of the event journalist Martin Smith commented, "Yesterday Don Valley welcomed their Satanic Majesties with 80-degree heat, a 50000 crowd and an atmosphere to bottle and sell.

People were impressed….and they loved the Stones.

It was virtually impossible not to, though early in the show one or two songs did show their age.

But before the end of a very long night, they won us all over.

By the time it was dark the doubters had been swept along by the energy and raw power of the grandads who redefined teenage rebellion thirty years ago.

Mick still sparks defiance and aggression, Ron and Keith are still among the best and Charlie looks patient and plays drums.

The set was outrageous beyond belief and at £20 for a T-shirt and £2 a pint, so were the prices.

But if anyone is worth £30 a ticket, it's The Rolling Stones.

And that's from a Beatles man."

The newspaper highlighted that 30000 burgers and hotdogs and 200000 drinks were consumed.

Merchandising sales were strong - for the tour it was reported they were expected to bring in £20 million.

And in the four-page special there was a section on "What The Fans Thought" - "In 1963 outraged parents locked up their daughters when the Stones were in town.

Long-haired, glassy-eyed and twitching with testosterone they were just too hot for a generation brought up on Perry Como and Mantovani.

But yesterday the teenagers of 30 years ago stood arm in arm with their own girls in the Attercliffe sunshine…

"I've been a fan of theirs since they first started but I never saw them back then, my mum wouldn't let me go," said Dorothy Flint whose 24-year-old-daughter bought them both tickets.

"It shows how much things have changed, my mum thought they were quite disgusting. She only liked quiet lads."

Helena Armstrong, 37, of Hunters Bar, Sheffield said: "We had to come. We might not be alive the next time they play here."

Gordon Mellor, aged 47, from Congleton, said, "I knew they'd do a proper job tonight. I saw them in 1963 but I can't remember where. It's too long ago."

On the front page of the following morning's *Yorkshire Post* a photo of Mick Jagger from the previous evening with the simple headline, "Stones roll back the years and give crowd satisfaction".

A full-page review in the *New Musical Express*, John Harris observed, "Within minutes of their arrival these four gnarled warhorses present their audience with irrefutable proof of their undimmed majesty...and through it all, you revel in the quiet delight that comes from not knowing how they manage to do it...Why if Mick Jagger should be amongst the 12 most irritating men on the planet does he carry tonight with an authority that's unimpeachable?"

That's a reviewer's take on proceedings – for the tens of thousands in the audience it was quite simply a fantastic show.

The set-list for the show (in order) – *Not Fade Away, You Got Me Rocking, It's All Over Now, Live With Me, Sparks Will Fly, (I Can't Get No) Satisfaction, Beast of Burden, Angie, Like A Rolling Stone, Rock And A Hard Place, Gimme Shelter, I Go Wild, Miss You, Honky Tonk Women, Connection, Slipping Away, Sympathy For The Devil, Street Fighting Man, Start Me Up, It's Only Rock 'n' Roll (But I Like It), Brown Sugar (*Encore*), Jumpin' Jack Flash (*Encore*)*

Mick Jagger made the band introductions after *Honky Tonk Women*, returning for *Sympathy for the Devil*. Keith Richards on lead vocals for *Connection* and *Slipping Away*.

They were on stage for just over two hours.

After the show Dad picked us up in the car about a half mile from the venue and we were back in Gleadless by 11.30pm that night.

It meant a very late drive home to Guildford – M1 and part of the M25. No roadworks, smooth journey. Little traffic at that time of night. Not as conscious of my speed as I should have been – lights flashed from the newly installed traffic cameras on the M25.

Thankfully no letter received about speeding – maybe they were just testing the flashing lights! It would have spoiled an otherwise fabulous night.

Support act for the show that night was provided by Scottish band Del Amitri.

Many years later Del Amitri's front man, Justin Currie, reflected on the show supporting the Stones in Sheffield on BBC Radio 2's Ken Bruce Show (May 2021) in the "Tracks of Their Years" slot (one of his track selections the Stones' *Happy*),

"I have to pick a Rolling Stones' song, I mean not just because they are a massive influence on anybody that writes songs vaguely in the rock genre, but we had pals, a rock band called "Gun" that were on the same label as us, on A&M in the 90s, and they had done a big long month, month and a half, long tour with the Stones in Europe in the mid-90s, and they came off the road just going, "You've got to support the Stones, they're totally amazing, they just treat you like royalty"

And they told us all these stories about how you go to your dressing room on the first day and the Stones go, "What are you doing in your dressing room, you're in our dressing room".

So, they've got this whole philosophy that the world outside of their bubble is the enemy, whereas if you're in the tent you're just one of them.

So, we did one show with them, in Sheffield, and they got us a police escort to the venue, which we'd never had before which was a complete riot. They let you use any bit of the production you wanted, there were no limitations on what you could use in terms of the PA and lights. And they literally just say, "You're with us, you're with us for the day", and you get everything they get.

They just treat you like princes…."

What Mr. Currie did not mention was their own performance on the day – or rather the culmination of their performance as the support act. It was a capable, easy-listening performance prior to the main act.

Nothing special but perfectly satisfactory. Thanking the audience for their (polite) applause the front man said something I've not heard before or since from a support act at a show,

"Would you like an encore?"

The audience seemed momentarily stunned by the question.

What his thinking was in asking it I really don't know. It took "balls"/stupidity/warped humour/temerity or maybe a combination of all those to ask that question.

A strong and unequivocal response from the audience – most definitely in the negative to his suggestion. The negative ranged from "No", laced with some choice anglo-saxon words, to a crescendo of booing from a goodly number in the crowd.

Mr. Currie immediately recognised his time was up – hastily departing with the accurate, if obvious, observation that "You're here for the main act." Too right.

The next date on the tour was two days later at Wembley Stadium London.

The Rolling Stones' LP, *Voodoo Lounge*, released on 11th July 1994, it reached number 1 and won the inaugural Grammy Award for best Rock Album in 1995, it stayed on the chart for 34 weeks.

The Rolling Stones single, *I Go Wild*, released on 3rd July 1995, reached number 29 and stayed in the chart for 3 weeks.

The *Sheffield Star* had increased in price to 26p and was now a tabloid sized newspaper.

And the headline on the front page on the evening of the show, "Man dies in flats blast" – reports of one man dying, four others injured and 200 evacuated following a gas leak which resulted in "a massive gas explosion at a block of flats in Derbyshire" where the two-year-old flats were reduced to rubble. The flats were in Ilkeston, Derbyshire.

Chapter 11

Sunday 6 June 1999

Don Valley Stadium

Castrol presents….

The Bridges to Babylon tour opened in the USA on 23 September 1997 in Chicago and finished on 19th September 1998 in Istanbul, Turkey. A total of 97 shows – in the USA, Europe, South America and Asia.

Originally there were four British dates scheduled for August 1998 as part of the European leg of the tour – the Don Valley show set for 26 August 1998.

Chancellor of the Exchequer, Gordon Brown, put the kibosh on that! His tax reforms in the budget meant that the band would be significantly out of pocket if they went ahead with the dates in 1998 – reportedly leaving them with a £12 million tax bill.

The four dates of the British leg were hastily rearranged for June 1999 – Edinburgh, Sheffield and two dates at Wembley, together with an additional date at the much smaller Shepherds Bush Empire.

The changes to the tour schedule for tax reasons caused a great furore.

Newspaper cartoonists took their opportunity – "I Don't Need No Self-Assessment" says the frontman in one cartoon, and in another introducing the band, "And on keyboard, tax consultant. Kevin Botley."

Mick Jagger was reported as saying, "We would have expected the new rules to have applied at the end of the year, not to take effect in the middle. If we did the UK shows it would have meant the entire European tour ran at a loss."

He explained, "A Rolling Stones world tour is a two-year project and there are over 200 people involved. I'm really sorry and apologetic to all those who who've now got to wait until next year to see the shows."

Eleven European dates were scheduled for summer 1999 – this brief tour opening in Stuttgart on May 29th and concluding in Cologne on June 20th visiting five different countries. It was reported that 519000 fans had attended the eleven shows with a reported gross revenue of $25 million. 10 outdoor shows with the largest reported attendance at Groningen in the Netherlands – 75000. Don Valley had a reported attendance of 32400.

This tour followed the No Security tour which opened at the beginning of that year in Oakland, USA on 25th January and played 40 shows in North America finishing in San Jose on 20 April.

The combined North American and European tours in 1999 reportedly grossed $88.5 million revenue with over one million tickets sold.

General admission tickets for Don Valley were £30.

As the Don Valley date approached the music paper *New Musical Express* simply stated in its Gig Guide that The Rolling Stones/Sheryl Crow were playing at the Don Valley Stadium on 6 June with the venue's telephone number.

The music paper's rival, *Melody Maker,* provided the same information and additionally offered this observation, "The Rolling Stones Decrepit old f***ers….."

No doubt very many would take issue with these slurs – including me! It will no doubt have come as a disappointment to *Melody Maker* and its then readers that it ceased to exist after 2000 – whilst The Rolling Stones continued to enjoy decades more recording and touring. I think it safe to say *Melody Maker* was very wide of the mark.

Once again, *The Star* took the lead in setting the scene for their Sheffield performance.

On the night before the show the headline – "Get ready to rock at Don Valley – "Small army sets stage for Stones". It reported, "A huge army of workers were today transforming Don Valley Stadium into rock 'n' roll theatre for tomorrow's Rolling Stones gig.

Over 200 professional roadies, permanently touring with the Stones across the world, are creating rock 'n' roll razzmatazz.

And about 200 more lucky locals from South Yorkshire, who volunteered their services to Stones tour managers, were allowed to build the massive stage set.

The entourage also includes carpenters, riggers, make-up artists, caterers, drivers and security guards.

Giant statues, huge blow-up figures and an amazing backdrop of gold and silver will turn the sport's stadium into a colourful Babylon scene.

Tour promoter Steve Howard said, "We wouldn't be able to do this without the local help. Everyone likes to play a part in a Rolling Stones gig.

The steel skeleton has already been built and this took 15 trucks to transport the materials and equipment.

Another 34 trucks will be coming over the next day to build up the sound system and the massive 22-ton screen.

We think this is the best Rolling Stones set ever and it will take your breath away".

And then Steve revealed the Stones will be getting wet with the crowd if traditional Sheffield weather turns up, "Only a tiny roof will cover drummer Charlie Watts and the amplification system, leaving most of the band exposed to the elements."

Add to that the stage design included a 150 feet long telescoping bridge that extended from the main stage to a "B stage" positioned centrally on the pitch.

The whole area of logistics for a tour by the Rolling Stones had been growing exponentially with each new tour. The Bridges to Babylon tour the biggest tour to date.

A booklet for each member of the crew brought home the numbers, the detail and extent of the planning.

As well as those roles identified in the newspaper report there were – Production Manager/Accountant/Coordinator; Site Coordinators; Instrument Technicians; Lighting Technicians; Video Technicians; Sound Technicians; Camera Operators; Pyrotechnic Crew; Show Power Crew; Dressing Rooms Coordinator; Laundress; Merchandising Crew; Truck Drivers; Steel Crew and two members of the crew responsible for "Backstage Ambiance".

Tour Related Offices are specified and contact details referenced – their locations worldwide – the specified offices included those for Management – Prince Rupert Lowenstein Ltd in London; Tour Consultants; Business Management – Tour Production; Travel; Set Design – Engineering; Set – Curtains; Fiberglass (as spelt in the booklet); Inflatables; Staging; Lighting; Sound – Video; Pyrotechnics – Confetti; Power; Trucking – Buses; Freight – Shipping; Furnishings; Catering; Public Relations; Legal Representation; Merchandising; Itineraries; Radios; Cellulars; Insurance; Ticketing.

It was a massive operation.

Details on Load-In dates, travelling dates and times, rest dates, construction dates, hotel details and on it went.

Separate crews for different venues – Blue Crew, Green Crew, Red Crew.

At specific venues the booklet identified the precise time that – Doors Open; Support Band On-Stage; Set Change; Rolling Stones On Stage; Sunset; Curfew.

And underlining the detail in the booklet it gives guidance on using telephones in hotels including – "Time & Money saving tip: to make additional calls, do not hang up, but simply press the # and wait for the voice prompt. This will save on the hotel surcharge for the additional calls."

In the lead up to the Don Valley show *The Star* had a picture of Mick Jagger "On stage last night" as "Jagger and pals tune up for the city" – noting that "The Stones revved up for their Sheffield gig with an electrifying performance in Scotland last night (at Edinburgh's Murrayfield Stadium)."

The Sheffield show? The front page of *The Star* the day following the event had a picture of Mick Jagger wearing a long raincoat with the headline, "Jumpin' Jack Splash!", commenting that the frontman was "singing in the rain yesterday as thousands of Rolling Stones fans braved torrential downpours to see the band's triumphant return to Sheffield's Don Valley Stadium".

Paul License reported on events with the headline, "Stones reign in the rain and roll back the years".

He observed, "One day Mick Jagger's grandkids will groan as he pulls out his photo album. "This was the day our British fans showed how much they loved us," he'll repeat as he points to a Marathon Gate at Don Valley Stadium with a somewhat sodden reporter braving the downpour.

The picture was taken last night.

A couple of police outriders heralded the approach of the Rolling Stones' cavalcade. Four black limos and a couple of people carriers swept into the stadium.

The only thing different about the first limousine was that, as it approached the gate, its window wound down half a foot – not too much as it was pouring down with rain – and Mick Jagger popped his face forward and raised his camera.

The rain persisted for the next hour as final preparations were made for the Stones show...And then it grew heavier as Sheryl Crow and her band came out to warm up the crowd.

A few hot water bottles and some thermals would have been handy too. But all credit to Ms Crow. As the heavens bucketed down, she sang and played her heart out.

By the time Keith Richards led his mates out, the rain had stopped. But only for a while.

The band blasted straight into *Jumping Jack Flash*. It could have been Jumping Jack Splash. With puddles welling on the stage and stair-rod rainfall adding extra sparkle to the spotlights, the greatest rock and roll band in the world showed that they settle for no half measures in anything.

The stage was huge, the sound was thunderous, the lights were spectacular and it was all overshadowed by four guys who have been setting the music pace for generations.

The audience was a mix of young and less young. But it was mostly diehard Rolling Stones fans who have followed their idols through thick and thin and found themselves in the rain in the Don Valley Stadium and in the full flow of youth again as the Rolling Stones rolled back the years.

Highlight of the show came as the stage darkened and was stabbed by a fusillade of hypnotic blue lights.

A huge gantry snaked out over the heads of the crowd and came to rest at a tiny stage which rose up in the middle of the audience.

The band raced across and kicked off with *Route 66*, then *Like A Rolling Stone* followed by a blues set, which shrank the stadium to the dimensions of a pub's back room.

As the Stones returned to the main stage, Mick Jagger made his one concession of the night to the weather. He put on a mac and trilby. But the mac soon came off as he danced and dived around the hundreds of yards of stage.

The trilby, however, remained in place. After all, this is Sheffield. The band had just delivered the Full Monty and as anyone will tell you, you can leave your hat on here.

Two hours of non-stop energy, enthusiasm and expertise pass in the wink of an eye. The Rolling Stones may be easy targets for many but not one member of the stadium crowd could fault last night's show.

I Can't Get No Satisfaction was the encore. What an understatement! What a show."

What Mr. License's report does not mention is the build-up and opening to the show.

As usual with a Stones' show it was dramatic and spectacular – an eerie dying down of general noise in the crowd, video screens flickered into action….then footage of what looked like a grey, steel structure – possibly in an underground car park – all the video in black and white which added to the effect.

After about 20 seconds figures appear – four of them in the distance on the screen – the camera moves closer to the figures, Mick, Keith,

Charlie and Ron. They're focussed, concentrating, looking mean and cool at the same time. The guitarists with their instrument, Charlie with drumsticks in hand, Jagger puts on his sunglasses as they all walk towards the camera. A drum and cymbal backbeat to the walking figures.

They enter a cage-like lift – the crowd's noise heightening…the lift cage opens…the four men exit towards the front of the screen and then pow! As they came close to the video screen front – bang – there they were on stage.

Keith Richards' opening chords to *Jumping Jack Flash*. Charlie Watts at the drums and Ron Wood on guitar, followed some seconds later – and for yet more dramatic effect – the livewire frontman catapulting himself from rear to front of stage in the blink of an eye, arms gyrating, and skirting the front of the stage as he blasted out the opening lines of the song.

And the crowd as one – anticipation and expectation sated, we were off and running, with no thought for the weather.

That build-up and opening to their stage entry remains my favourite. There have been others more elaborate, brighter, louder, pyrotechnics to the fore. But that one was simple, to the point, the four subjects utterly focussed – for a minute the meanest looking guys on the planet – as the tension for the audience builds and then breaks with their stage entry. A minute and a half from video screen flickering into action to their dramatic bursting on stage.

We were on the pitch close to where the small stage was positioned – and certainly for us it was their arrival and performance on the "B" stage that was the highlight of the show. Jagger in leather jacket – 55 years old – and performing with the athleticism and exuberance of a man less than half his age. And his audience lapping it up, many joining as one to jump around and sing in sheer delight – me included.

And the rain….it rained…and it rained. No-one – least of all us – gave it a second thought.

In his first comments to the crowd after the second song Mick Jagger acknowledged the delay to the band playing in the UK – "Welcome everybody to Sheffield. Welcome to Don Valley…It's been really wonderful for you to wait such a long, long time for us to get here and we're very happy to see you here today. Thank you from all of us to all of you."

The frontman's other interactions with the audience included his observation that, "Sheffield's known for its choral ability…" as the prelude to the song *Saint of Me,* inviting the crowd to join in the chorus.

And he referenced the weather a number of times – first in his band introductions as he introduced the brass section, telling Kent Smith on trumpet to "come out from under that bloody umbrella." Smith's introduction was followed by, Michael Davies on trombone, Tim Ries on saxophone, Bobby Keyes on tenor sax. The crowd reaction to Keyes always the loudest for the brass section – he'd toured with the band since 1972, and the Texan went as far back as playing with Buddy Holly in their native state in the 1950s.

On vocals Bernard Fowler and Lisa Fischer, Blondie Chaplin on vocals and percussion, Chuck Leavell on keyboards and Darryl Jones on bass (guitar).

More references to the weather during the show and prior to the final song the frontman commented, "You're a bloody marvellous audience in all this rain I'll tell you that" and at the end prior to the encore, "Thank you very much Sheffield – you've been wonderful. Really appreciate it tonight everybody."

From our perspective we simply enjoyed the show, wrapped up in it, the experience, the sheer delight of the occasion. At the end we noticed we were more than a bit wet as a result of the rain. So what?

21 songs on the set-list, the Stones took to the stage at 8.50pm and were on for just over two hours.

The songs in order – *Jumping Jack Flash, You Got Me Rocking, Live With Me, Respectable, Gimme Shelter, Ruby Tuesday, Honky Tonk Women* (with Sheryl Crow)*, Saint Of Me, Out Of Control, Paint It Black, Before They Make Me Run, You Don't Have To Mean It, Route 66 (*B-stage*), Like A Rolling Stone (*B-stage*), Midnight Rambler (*B-stage*), Sympathy For The Devil, Tumbling Dice, It's Only Rock 'n' Roll, Start Me Up, Brown Sugar* (encore), *Satisfaction* (encore).

Mick Jagger made the band introductions after *Paint It Black* and then departed the stage returning for *Route 66* on the B-Stage.

Keith Richards on lead vocals for *Before They Make Me Run* and *You Don't Have To Mean It*.

The advent of new technology had produced websites for fans on the internet by the late 1990s – the show was heralded an unbridled success – this comment typical of many, "Amazing show despite the rain - The Rolling Stones were incredible in Sheffield."

A reported attendance of 32425 at the show.

And Kim Ward - wife of my school friend Brian Ward from Anns Road Infants days - recollects meeting Mick Jagger late one night on the eve of the Rolling Stones' show at the Don Valley Stadium.

At that time, she worked at the Stadium and was on a ladies' night out at Aston Hall (now a Best Western hotel located close to the Sheffield boundary and the M1 motorway) with friends Karen and Diane. Leaving the venue at close to midnight they approached the main doors - the doors were opened for them from the outside by none other than a casually dressed Mick Jagger.

Ever the gentleman he ushered them through, "Ladies first".

The three ladies thanked him and wished him well for the forthcoming show.

Acknowledging their good wishes with, "Thank you ladies I'm looking forward to it".

A chance encounter and one that has stayed with the three ladies ever since.

And it seems quite possible that Mick and maybe the other band members were staying at the venue - easy and quick access to the motorway and no more than 20 minutes' drive to the Don Valley Stadium.

The next date on the tour was in two days' time at the Shepherds Bush Empire London.

The Rolling Stones' LP, *Bridges To Babylon*, released on 29th November 1997, and reached number 6 in the chart and stayed on the chart for 22 weeks.

The Rolling Stones' single, *Out Of Control*, released on 10th August 1998, reached number 51 in the chart, and stayed on the chart for 2 weeks.

In other news the front page of *The Star* (increased in price to 30p) on the night before the show – the main headline – "Watery Grave" – the story of an anguished daughter" who "would rather dig up her mum's body than leave her lying in a sodden Sheffield grave". The plot in the Wisewood cemetery apparently often swamped by inches of water because of poor drainage.

Meanwhile on the sports pages of the newspaper that evening, disappointment reported for the Sheffield Eagles rugby league team – whose home ground was the Don Valley Stadium – having lost their game against Bradford Bulls 52-2. The beginning of James Collins' report on the game would not have endeared him to the Stones or their fans, "First you get turfed out of your home by geriatric rocker Mick Jagger…."

No one who had seen the show at the Don Valley Stadium would have used or recognised that adjective.

As a postscript BBC1's regional *Look North* programme had a feature on the show at the Don Valley Stadium – with a brief clip of the band in action. It prompted mother to acknowledge their longevity and that they could still pull in a crowd – "I'll give you that". For his part Dad chose not to participate in the discussion.

Chapter 12

Sunday 27 August 2006

Don Valley Stadium

American Express presents….

A Bigger Bang

Part of the "A Bigger Bang" tour which started in Boston, USA in August 2005 and finished two years later in August 2007 with three shows in London. 147 shows in total and reportedly grossing $558.3 million – the highest grossing tour of all time at the tour's completion.

In February 2006 – the band performed at the half-time interval of Super Bowl XL in Detroit followed later that month by the band giving a free concert on the Copacabana Beach in Rio De Janeiro – a reported 2 million people on the beach.

The British dates in August 2006 were two shows at London's Twickenham Stadium (originally intended to be at the newly rebuilt Wembley Stadium but the rebuilding work at Wembley took longer than anticipated), Hampden Park Glasgow, Don Valley Stadium Sheffield and the Millenium Stadium Cardiff.

Similar to other venues differential ticket prices applied based on position in the stadium – at the Don Valley Stadium the first rows from the stage £150 plus booking fee. We went for those tickets – fifteen rows from the front of the stage we were keen to get as close a view as possible in a large outdoor arena. Other tickets available at £90 and £60 plus booking fee.

Interesting to note on the reverse of the ticket there were ten "Terms and Conditions" specified – and at number 6. "This concert will take place after sundown. Please wear warm waterproof clothing. All pitch seating and much of the stands are uncovered and you will be exposed to the elements. Please be well prepared." Term and condition or not, in the event this was good advice.

And the final sentence on the reverse of the ticket in bold and in block capitals - **"WARNING: IT IS POSSIBLE THAT EXPOSURE TO LOUD MUSIC MAY CAUSE DAMAGE TO HEARING."**

None of the other tickets for previous shows in Sheffield had carried such a warning.

The show took place on the same day as Sheffield Wednesday played a Yorkshire derby against Leeds United in the city. My two passions in one day – Sheffield Wednesday and The Rolling Stones.

Wednesday lost, 2-1 – unluckily in many people's eyes. Disappointed but I'm sure the show would more than make up for it.

Paolo Nutini the support act for the show. Very few of the support acts I've seen at a Rolling Stones show have registered with me, and perhaps only The Specials in their home city of Coventry had made a real positive impact as a support act for me. The main act is my focus. This one no different – Paolo Nutini was fine but in my view nothing to get excited about.

Five days in advance of the show there was an article in *The Star* – "Warning to motorists over Stones concert" – including this piece of advice, "The wrinkly rockers are playing at the Don Valley Stadium and motorists are being warned to avoid the area between 3pm and 7pm".

We heeded that advice, and for the first time for a Don Valley show took the Supertram from Gleadless to the venue and return. It worked a treat. Little time waiting for a tram at either end – just needed to make sure that on the return journey we had the one with the destination board, Halfway.

In a preview for the show the *York Press* stated:

"To slightly misquote a famous old cliché: you can't keep an old man down.

If anyone was living proof of this, it has to be The Rolling Stones – a quartet of increasingly geriatric old rockers who have refused to let life get the upper hand.

Not laryngitis (Mick Jagger), being treated for throat cancer (Charlie Watts), or even having surgery to relieve a blood clot and swelling on the brain (Keith Richards) has been able to dim these old geezers' lust for life.

Despite everything, tour director Michael Cohl claims A Bigger Bang is on course to be The Stones "greatest tour yet".

"This band is redefining the concert experience," he said.

"There is nothing even comparable to the thrill of being on stage with the Rolling Stones and seeing a stadium show from the band's perspective.""

The *York Press* reported Paolo Nutini's comments, "This is a really exciting time for me. The band's support for me has been overwhelming and I am truly honoured to be asked to support again." (Nutini had supported earlier in the tour at the Ernst-Happel Stadium in Vienna).

Two days before the show there were still some tickets available - at £90 and £150 with ten per cent booking fee - from the Hallam FM Arena box office.

The Star printed its "Entertainment news and previews" section three days before the show with the headline, "It's only rugga roll...." – the reporter, David Dunn, had seen the opening night of the UK tour in London:

"It's big – very big – and it most certainly is clever.

Then you wouldn't expect anything less of the corporate rock t-rex that is The Rolling Stones.

"We should have been at Wembley " said Jagger to a damp Twickenham, but I reckon they should have that finished in time for the Arctic Monkeys farewell tour" (Arctic Monkeys a Sheffield band).

And this vast venue in a leafy London suburb easily catered for the multi-storey stage set the Stones had as their playground. A cross between an NCP car park and a space-craft, this impressive structure incorporated competition winners as well as the well-heeled as part of its function, as they waved down at the band from behind.

With a back-drop of giant screens and more lights than a Heathrow runway, the Stones lit up the night sky with a display befitting a resilient global rock institution, well drilled by time and bolstered by high finance.

They opened this UK leg of this 5-stadium tour with guaranteed crowd-pleasers *Jumpin' Jack Flash* and *Brown Sugar* and waded into a set bristling with hits and laboured only by a couple of the mandatory newer album tracks.

Jagger, who recently had to pull out of a Spanish show because of laryngitis, displays as much energy as he's ever had, an almost constantly fidgeting string bean of a man flitting from one side of the stage to the other, over-looked by a towering jumbo screen image of himself, Messrs Richards, Watts and Wood and that omnipresent Andy Warhol tongue.

Accompanied by a match-fit bunch of musicians and singers and one of the most expensive looking stages to be devised for the UK, there's very little here for even the most casual of fans to grumble about.

The Stones may not roll quite as quickly as they once did – what with veteran guitarists falling out of coconut trees (a reference to Keith Richards) and all – but they still know how to shake a stadium.

Don Valley be prepared."

The Don Valley show was the 94th of the "A Bigger Bang" tour.

And the official logo for the tour was the so-called "Chippy Tongue" – an exploding re-design of the tongue and lips logo.

The stage for the tour designed by Mark Fisher – production design by Fisher, Mick Jagger, Charlie Watts and Patrick Woodroffe.

The show included state-of-the-art electronics that presented visual screen shots of the Stones tongue and live footage.

Height of the stage was 84 feet. And the multi-level construction included balconies behind the stage with accommodation for 400 members of the audience.

And a section of the stage detached itself and took the entire band along a catwalk, creating a separate B stage in the middle of the stadium.

We were prepared – Gates opened at 4.30pm – me and my brother had seen the football at lunchtime and made our way by public transport to the Don Valley stadium arriving at close to 7pm.

Our seats guaranteed close to the stage so we took time to check out the merchandising stalls – the obligatory T-Shirt purchased, black and it seemed pricey at £25, but a necessary souvenir of the event. Again, it represented a good advert for The Rolling Stones and American Express.

Locating our position close to the stage we were 15 rows from the front and right of centre of the stage as we looked at it. Certainly, a good view, and no reliance on the giant video screens erected behind and at the sides of the stage.

As always – for me at least – the build-up to the band coming on stage and making their entrance was a particular highlight. Light men had climbed their gantry, music tape had stopped, noise building, noise heightened...fireworks reached up to the sky from behind the back of the stage coupled with computer-generated graphics representing the literal Big Bang on the huge video screens.

Faces of the four band members appear hazily on the screens, followed by more graphics depicting fast travel through a city's streets – then cue Keith Richards on the screen playing the opening notes of *Jumping Jack Flash*. We're off and certainly running...Jagger appears centre-stage – dressed in a sequined purple jacket...moving like a whirling dervish, the centre of attention, the central attraction, eyes inevitably drawn towards him as he dominates the stage by dint of his presence, his movement, his sheer energy.

It was another fabulous show with the lighting and pyrotechnics an integral feature complementing the performers on stage.

In that context Charlie Watts had observed, "We became very aware of not being seen – of just being there like ants. Mick is the one who has to project himself over the footlights. And when the show gets that big you need a little extra help...you need fireworks, you need lights. You need a bit of theatre."

Perhaps the highlight of the show was the "B-stage" detaching from the main stage and under its own propulsion taking the performers 100 metres and more towards the centre of the stadium. Whoops of delight from the audience as the stage first detached and then set in motion. Noise increasing as the stage progressed further into the crowd. No running across a bridge to the B-stage on this tour. The technical wizardry had gone up another level.

Rain again a feature of this show and the adverse weather perhaps quietened the audience a little. The stage crew busied themselves with sweeping water from the stage and laying carpet. The performers on stage? – they carried on doing what they do best – playing their music and putting on a show – a great show. Indeed, if anything, the rain seemed to galvanise them even more to produce a memorable show.

And the rain was a theme of Mick Jagger's engagement with the crowd through the show – after they played *Streets of Love* he observed, "How you doing out there? It's getting very slippery".

The rain continued and after *It's Only Rock 'n' Roll* – "Well it wasn't supposed to rain was it? Dancing up here is like dancing with beer on the dancefloor, you know what I mean?"

During his band introductions and that of backing vocalist Lisa Fischer he said, "Don't let the rain get your hair down girl".

On Keith Richards' introduction to the audience the latter commented, "Hi Sheffield. How you doing? Sorry it's raining but some things you can't do."

Jagger's opening line with his audience, "It's great to be back in Sheffield everybody, it feels good to be here."

He went on to compliment the city as a sporting one and said, "Congratulations to United getting back to the Premiership after 12 years…Def Leppard are from here right. We're going to do our version of *Pour Some Sugar On Me* after or should it be the *Greasy Chip Butty* song?"

Audience reaction to his highlighting United was mixed – hardly surprising given the nature of the football rivalry in the city…support for Wednesday and United as partisan as any in the country. His referencing the *Greasy Chip Butty* song (based on the tune of *Annie's*

Song by John Denver) and sung passionately by the red and white supporters received no audible reaction from his audience. He made no reference to Wednesday or their supporters' song, Hi Ho Sheffield Wednesday (based on Jeff Beck's *Hi Ho Silver Lining*).

Given my football allegiance, for the first and only time I was not impressed with Mick's words to his audience.

To the newspapers and their perspective on the show - The *Yorkshire Post* had a photo of the front man on the front page with the headline – "SATISFACTION: Jack Flash is still jumping" and commented, "A sequin-suited Mick Jagger and the rest of the Rolling Stones treated a sell-out 35000 crowd to a vintage performance last night. "

Inside a report by Chris Bond under the headline – "Storming Stones roll back the years" – "Evergreen rock legend the Rolling Stones turned back the clock with a vintage performance at Sheffield's Don Valley Stadium last night.

The Stones are famous for their lavish stage shows and they did not disappoint adoring fans who witnessed a barnstorming concert from a band who have been defining music for more than 40 years.

Decked out in a purple sequinned jacket Sir Mick Jagger kicked off the gig with a belting version of *Jumpin' Jack Flash*, accompanied by a massive fireworks display.

Last night's show was the latest stop in their A Bigger Bang European tour and reinforced their position as the most famous band in the world.

Fans flocked in from all over the world. Computer expert David Slezak and his wife Stephanie travelled all the way from Seattle in the United States just to watch them.

"I went to 40 shows in eight countries on their last tour", Mrs Slezak said.

"We listen to a lot of new music but nobody gets close to them. They are the greatest band ever, there was nobody better before them and there has been nobody better since".

Many of those at last night's show have been fans since the 1960s, but this was far from a golden oldies convention. PhD students Ainsley McIntosh, and her friend Sally Newsome, from Halifax, are both in their 20s. They reckon the band is what rock and roll is all about.

"You see some bands today and they won't be around in five years, never mind 40," said Ainsley.

The Stones have seen it and done it all. They are survivors. People like Jimi Hendrix aren't around anymore, but they are still here and they're brilliant".

It seems Sir Mick and company just keep on going and time has not withered their music or huge popularity."

Meanwhile *The Star* had, "Satisfaction guaranteed as old 'uns refuse to fade away….", Andrew Foley reporting:

"For more than 30 years they've been the world's greatest tribute band.

After a string of classic singles, the band reached its zenith with Beggars Banquet, Let It Bleed, Sticky Fingers and Exile On Main Street – volumes one to four of all you need to know about rock music, and a brilliant consistency even the Beatles couldn't claim to match.

Then the records went a bit pear-shaped and Mick developed a taste for prancing about in stadiums and tight clothes.

We've been there ever since.

They are still playing *Sway, Sympathy For The Devil, Tumbling Dice* and *You Can't Always Get What You Want*. However, they do it ever so well.

Top price tickets were going for more than four times the £150 asking price but Stones gigs are big business for everyone.

After all, someone has to pay for the stage set, which is a cross between 60s tower block and Fritz Lang's Metropolis. There were bangs, fireworks and flames among the lights, walkways and giant screens.

They opened with *Jumpin' Jack Flash* and Jagger came out quicker than a boxer who needs to win in the first.

He's the ultimate entertainer who wrote the book on showmanship. It rained, heavy at times, but he wasn't put off, almost saying. "You've paid your cash, you get the same 100 per cent".

Keith Richards seemed genuinely happy to be there. He's probably happy to be anywhere after a lifetime of using his body as a chemical laboratory.

This a man who didn't so much sell his soul to the Devil – he drank Lucifer under the table before kicking his satanic hide out the door.

Charlie Watts sat at the back in a perspex box, giving minimum effort for maximum reward. He's been the engine room for more than 40 years. Nothing flash. Job done.

Ronnie Wood wove with Keith, trading guitar lines and swapping smiles as they avoided several near-miss collisions.

A section of the stage extended out into the middle of the crowd and they played *Honky Tonk Women* with the rain bouncing off the floor.

But it all passed too quickly. Suddenly it was that riff, Mick's lack of satisfaction and they were gone, until next time."

The *York Press* review:

"Don't be daft. The "best pub band in the world" still defy all before them: the calcifying ravages of age and the fickle flicker of pop fashions; Keith's brain surgery; a dearth of Top Ten singles for two decades; even Keith flouting Glasgow's smoking ban last Friday in what passes for latter-day rock rebellion.

On Sunday, as if countering the Stones' shooting flames and fireworks that lit up the night with a bigger bang, Sheffield's industrial skies threw all they could at Sir Michael Jagger and his 35,000 subjects.

Here was unexpected extra drama, far removed from the sunshine glamour of playing Rio or Rome, as minions scurried for carpeting to make the stage safe. "They're doing the kitchen next," joked Jagger. Ever the dandy, he reached for a hat then another, so did Ronnie and dear Keef, whose peaked cap with a pirate motif winked knowingly at Johnny Depp's Captain Jack tribute.

Charlie Watts, the old father time of the drums, played on under a protective plastic shield, as the band were propelled forward on a mobile mini-stage to the heart of the audience in the furious rain.

This was a direct parallel with their only rival as the world's greatest stadium show band, U2, and it was the only occasion they were found wanting by not making more of the more intimate setting.

The ageless anthems and stadium style remain the same, with the familiar format of a couple of new numbers (*Streets of Love* surpassing the strutting rock of *Rough Justice*): a lesser-known oldie (*Sway*); a ropey vocal interlude for Keef and the inevitable farewell of *Satisfaction* guaranteed as they still reign in the rain."

A bootleg recording of the show was produced entitled "Pour Some Sugar On Sheffield" – words referenced by Mick Jagger during the show – a reference to the song by Sheffield band Def Leppard.

The Stones were on stage for 2 hours the set-list, in order – *Jumping Jack Flash, Start Me Up, She's So Cold, Let's Spend The Night Together, Sway, Streets Of Love, Bitch, It's Only Rock 'n' Roll, Tumbling Dice, Slipping Away, Before They Make Me Run, Miss You, Rough Justice, Get Off Of My Cloud, Honky Tonk Women, Sympathy For The Devil, Brown Sugar, You Can't Always Get What You Want, Satisfaction.*

After Mick Jagger's band introductions following *Tumbling Dice*, he left the stage for the next two numbers – Keith Richards on lead vocals for *Slipping Away* and *Before They Make Me Run*.

Miss You, Rough Justice and *Get Off Of My Cloud,* and *Honky Tonk Women* were played on the B-stage.

You Can't Always Get What You Want and *Satisfaction* were the two songs for the encore.

Since the 1999 show fan websites on the internet had increased. For this 2006 show the reaction one of near universal acclaim including, "Really enjoyable concert…despite the rain they seemed to play better and better and the memories will last forever.".

A reported 34034 attendance at the show.

The next date on the tour was in two days' time at the Millenium Stadium Cardiff.

The Rolling Stones LP, *A Bigger Bang*, released on 5th September 2005 and reached number 2 in the charts, staying in the chart for 14 weeks.

The Rolling Stones' single, *Biggest Mistake*, released on 10th June 2006 and reached number 51 in the chart and stayed in the chart for 2 weeks.

The front page of *The Star* (now 30p) on the Saturday before the show – "Two Dead In Plane Tragedy" – "Drivers see aircraft crash into field and burst into flames" – the pilot and passenger in the single engine light aircraft died when it crashed into a field adjacent to the M18 motorway near Rotherham.

Chapter 13

Since 2006….

The Rolling Stones have continued with their huge and highly successful tours.

The *50 & Counting* tour of Europe and North America in 2012 and 2013 celebrated the 50th anniversary of the band's formation – 30 shows – two venues in Great Britain – Hyde Park and headlining at Glastonbury.

14 On Fire in 2014 – 29 shows in Asia, Europe and Oceania – no shows in Great Britain.

2015 and the *Zip Code* tour of North America – 17 shows.

February 2016 and the start of their Latin American tour – 14 shows in a seven-week period culminating in a free open-air concert in Havana, Cuba attended by an estimated 500000.

A major exhibition dedicated to the band – *Exhibitionism* – took place in 2016, initially at the Saatchi Gallery in London and then taken to various major cities around the world.

The *No Filter* tour covered a four-year period starting in September 2017 in Hamburg, Germany – then interrupted by the Covid pandemic – 58 shows in Europe and North America. In Great Britain shows in London at the London Stadium and Twickenham, Southampton, Coventry, Manchester, Edinburgh and Cardiff.

In 2022 a tour of Europe – *Sixty* – to celebrate the 60th anniversary of the band's formation. This one without drummer Charlie Watts who passed away in October 2021. Steve Jordan taking his place. 14 shows in total – 3 in Great Britain, at Liverpool and two shows at Hyde Park, London.

Output of new music over this time has been limited – releasing the album *Blues and Lonesome* in 2016 – an album of covers. It was received to critical acclaim and success in the charts.

There have been several releases on DVD and CD of their live shows – including *Grrr, The Biggest Bang, Havana Moon* and more.

Films have been released – the excellent Martin Scorsese directed *Shine a Light* in 2008 and the critically acclaimed documentary style *Crossfire Hurricane* (2012).

The band continues to record – a new album, *Hackney Diamonds*, released in October 2023, and they have plans for further tours.

250 million albums sold to date, blazing the trail for bands to follow, their impact has been simply immense. Musically, culturally the Rolling Stones are at the forefront.

Looking back over sixty and more years their success and longevity is quite simply amazing.

Chapter 14

Venues

City Hall

Located in Barker's Pool in the city centre.

Designed in 1920 by E. Vincent Harris construction was delayed because of the economic climate in that decade. The works commenced in 1929, undertaken and completed by local contractor, George Longden & Son.

The City Hall was officially opened on 22 September 1932.

In 1916 it was proposed as a Memorial Hall to commemorate the dead of the First World War, but by the time of its completion its name had changed to Sheffield City Hall.

It is a building in the neo-classical style and has a giant portico.

The Oval Hall is the largest hall in the building with a seated capacity of 2271; within the building the Memorial Hall has a seated capacity of 425 and the Ballroom a seated capacity of 400.

The Rolling Stones shows took place in the Oval Hall.

Performers at the City Hall have included Nat King Cole, Louis Armstrong, Jerry Lee Lewis, Johnny Mathis, The Beatles and Acker Bilk.

The City Hall is now a Grade ll listed building.

Gaumont Theatre

The building was originally named The Regent Theatre, and built for the Provincial Cinematograph Theatres circuit (PCT). It was the first major cinema designed by architect William Edward Trent. It was located in Barker's Pool, diagonally opposite the City Hall.

It opened on December 26th 1927 with seating for 2300 – 1450 in the stalls and 850 in the balcony.

The Neo-Classical/Italian Renaissance style auditorium was very similar to Thomas Lamb designed theatres in the USA. There was a double dome in the ceiling with the projection box built into the dome. The cinema had full stage facilities, including a Wurlitzer 2Manual/8Rank theatre organ.

PCT were taken over by Gaumont British Theatres in 1929 – the name Regent retained until 27th July 1946 when it was re-named Gaumont Theatre.

The stage was used by a range of artists in the 1960s – as well as The Rolling Stones, Duane Eddy, Eddie Cochran, Bobby Darin, Victor Borg, Nina & Frederick, The Beatles and the Count Basie Orchestra.

In October 1968 the Gaumont closed – the original decoration removed and less than a year later two curtain-walled auditoriums opened on 23rd July 1969 – seating 737 in the former balcony and 1150 in the former stalls. A third screen was opened in 1979 in the former café area which seated 144.

The Gaumont closed for the last time on 7th November 1985 and demolition began the following month.

Offices and a twin screen Odeon Cinema were built on the site. The new cinema opened in 1987 (seating 500 and 324 respectively) and closed in 1994. It was replaced by a night club.

Don Valley Stadium

A sports stadium in the east end of the city.

The venue was completed in September 1990 and hosted the 1991 World Student Games. It was named after the nearby River Don and valley.

The stadium has been used for athletics, football, rugby league and American football as well as hosting music events.

At the time of its closure, Don Valley Stadium was the second largest athletics stadium in the UK behind the London Olympic Stadium.

15000 spectators could be accommodated on the open terrace with a seated capacity of 10000, giving an overall capacity of 25000 for sports events. For music events the stadium had 15000 seated and a maximum capacity of 50000 if the field was used to accommodate standing fans.

The Don Valley Stadium cost £29 million, and was the first new outdoor sporting venue built in the UK since Wembley Stadium (opened in 1923), when it was completed.

The first rock concert held at the stadium was by Sheffield band, Def Leppard.

The Rolling Stones' three performances at the venue are a record for a single artist. Other artists to have performed at the venue include Bon Jovi, U2, Michael Jackson, Tina Turner, Spice Girls, Celine Dion and the Red Hot Chilli Peppers.

The stadium was demolished in 2013 – the Olympic Legacy Park has been constructed on the site.

Bibliography

Sheffield Star newspaper

Sheffield Telegraph newspaper

Yorkshire Post newspaper

York Press

News of the World newspaper

New Musical Express

Melody Maker

Record Mirror

Disc Weekly

Radio Times, 23-29 August 2003

Awopbopaloobop Alopbamboom, Nik Cohn, Paladin, 1970

Revolt Into Style, George Melly, Penguin, 1972

Beyond Reason, Margaret Trudeau, Arrow Books, 1980

Stone Alone, Bill Wyman with Ray Coleman, Viking, 1990

The Rolling Stones 1962-1995 The Ultimate Guide, Felix Aeppli, Record Information Services, 1996

King of Clubs, Peter Stringfellow with Fiona Lafferty, Little, Brown And Company, 1996

The Rolling Stones A Life On The Road, Dora Loewenstein and Jools Holland, Virgin Books, 1998

Rolling With The Stones, Bill Wyman with Richard Havers, Dorling Kindersley, 2002

Stu, Will Nash, Out-Take Limited, 2003

Joe Cocker The Authorised Biography, J P Bean, Virgin Books, 2003

The Rolling Stones Off The Record, Mark Paytress, Omnibus Press, 2003

The Stones A History In Cartoons, Bill Wyman, Sutton Publishing, 2006

365 Days The Rolling Stones, Simon Wells, Abrams, 2008

Rolling Thru The Stones, Keno, Onek Publishing, 2009

Dave Berry All There Is To Know, Dave Berry with Mike Firth, Heron Publications, 2010

The Beatles vs The Rolling Stones, Jim Derogatis and Greg Kot, Voyageur Press, 2010

The Rolling Stones 50, Mick Jagger, Keith Richards, Charlie Watts, Ronnie Wood, Thames & Hudson, 2012

The Great Illustrated British Rolling Stones Discography 1963-2013, Julian Hardiman, Maus Of Music, 2014

You Had To Be There The Rolling Stones 1962-69, Richard Houghton, Gottahavebooks, 2015

The Rolling Stones In Concert, 1962-82, Ian M. Rusten, McFarland and Company, 2018

Hot Stuff The Story Of The Rolling Stones Through The Ultimate Memorabilia Collection, Matt Lee, Welbeck, 2021

The Rolling Stones in the Sixties A People's History, Richard Houghton, Spenwood Books, 2022

Start Me Up And Keep Me Growing, Berthold Bar-Bouysierre, Anthem Press, 2022

The Rolling Stones Essentials, MOJO Collectors' Series, 2023